"You Ready To Walk Down The Aisle In A White Dress, Promise To Love And Honor Me, Then Kiss Me And Throw A Bouquet?"

As Cole outlined the scenario, an unexpected vision bloomed in his mind. Sydney in a white dress. Sydney in a veil. Sydney with a spray of delicate roses trembling in her hands. He could feel her skin, smell her perfume, taste the sweetness of her lush lips.

"We'd both know it was fake," she said.

Cole startled out of the vision and gave a short nod. "Yeah. Right. We'd both know it was fake."

"And that's what would matter. That's what would count." She squared her shoulders. "Knowing the benefits, I could do it."

"Then so can I," said Cole, just as he'd known he would from the second his brother conceived the plan. His family needed him, and that was all that needed to be said.

Dear Reader,

Why not make reading Silhouette Desire every month your New Year's resolution? It's a lot easier—and a heck of a lot more enjoyable—than diet or exercise!

We're starting 2006 off with a bang by launching a brand-new continuity: THE ELLIOTTS. The incomparable Leanne Banks gives us a glimpse into the lives of this high-powered Manhattan family, with *Billionaire's Proposition.* More stories about the Elliotts will follow every month throughout the year.

Also launching this month is Kathie DeNosky's trilogy, THE ILLEGITIMATE HEIRS. Three brothers born on the wrong side of the blanket learned they are destined for riches. The drama begins with *Engagement between Enemies.* *USA TODAY* bestselling author Annette Broadrick is back this month with *The Man Means Business,* a boss/secretary book with a tropical setting and a sensual story line.

Rounding out the month are great stories with heroes to suit your every mood. Roxanne St. Claire gives us a bad boy who needs to atone for *The Sins of His Past.* Michelle Celmer gives us a dedicated physical therapist who is not above making a few late-night *House Calls.* And Barbara Dunlop (who is new to Desire) brings us a sexy cowboy whose kiss is as shocking as a *Thunderbolt over Texas.*

Here's to keeping that New Year's resolution!

Melissa Jeglinski

Melissa Jeglinski
Senior Editor

BARBARA DUNLOP

Thunderbolt over Texas

Published by Silhouette Books
America's Publisher of Contemporary Romance

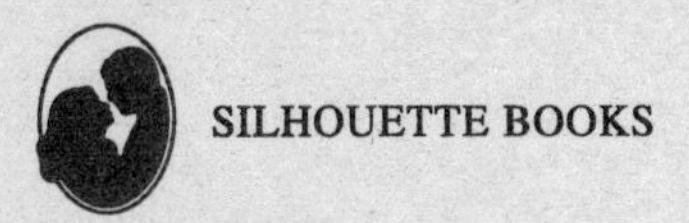

ISBN 0-373-76704-8

THUNDERBOLT OVER TEXAS

This edition published by arrangement with Harlequin Books S.A.

Visit Silhouette Books at www.eHarlequin.com

Printed in U.S.A.

Books by Barbara Dunlop

Silhouette Desire

Thunderbolt over Texas #1704

Harlequin Temptation

Forever Jake #848
Next to Nothing! #901
Too Close To Call #940
Flying High #1006
High Stakes #1010

Harlequin Flipside

Out of Order #22

Harlequin Duets

The Mountie Steals a Wife #54
A Groom in Her Stocking #90
The Wish-List Wife #98

BARBARA DUNLOP

writes romantic stories while curled up in a log cabin in Canada's far north, where bears outnumber people and it snows six months of the year. Fortunately, she has a brawny husband and two teenage children to haul firewood and clear the driveway while she sips cocoa and muses about her upcoming chapters. Barbara loves to hear from readers. You can contact her through her Web site at www.barbaradunlop.com.

For Angela of the Vikings.
Princess and Warrior.

One

Most people loved a good wedding.

Cole Erickson hated them.

It wasn't that he had anything against joy and bliss, or anything in particular against happily-ever-after. It was the fact that white dresses, seven-tiered cakes and elegant bouquets of roses reminded him that he'd failed countless generations of Ericksons and had broken more than a few hearts along the way.

So, as the recessional sounded in the Blue Earth Valley Church, and as his brother, Kyle, and Kyle's new bride, Katie, glided back down the aisle, Cole's smile was strained. He tucked the empty ring box into the breast pocket of his tux, took the arm of the maid of honor and followed the happy couple through the anteroom and onto the porch.

Outside, they were greeted by an entire town of well-wishers raining confetti and taking up the newly coined tradition of blowing bubbles at the bride and groom.

Somebody shoved a neon-orange bottle of bubble mix into Cole's hand. Emily, the freckle-faced maid of honor, laughed and released his arm, unscrewing the cap on her bottle and joining in the bubble cascade.

Grandma Erickson shifted to stand next to Cole. She waved away his offer of the bubble solution, but threw a handful of confetti across the wooden steps.

"Extra two hundred for the cleanup," she said.

"Only happens once in a lifetime," Cole returned, even though the soap and shredded paper looked more messy than festive.

"I've been meaning to talk to you about that."

Cole could feel his grandmother's lecture coming a mile away. "Grandma," he cautioned.

"Melanie was a nice girl."

"Melanie was a terrific girl," he agreed.

"You blew that one."

"I did." Grandma would get no argument from Cole. He'd loved Melanie. Everyone had loved Melanie. There wasn't a mean or selfish bone in her body, and any man on the planet would be lucky to have her as a wife.

Problem was, Cole had plenty of mean and selfish bones in his body. He couldn't be the husband Melanie or anyone else needed. He couldn't do the doting bridegroom, couldn't kowtow to a woman's whims, change his habits, his hair or his underwear style to suit another person.

In short, there was no way in the world he was getting married now or anytime in the foreseeable future. Which left him with one mother of a problem. A nine-hundred-year-old problem.

"You're not getting any younger," said Grandma.

"I've been thinking," said Cole as Kyle and Katie climbed into a chauffeur-driven limousine for the ten-mile ride back to the ranch and the garden reception.

"About time." Grandma harrumphed.

"I was thinking the Thunderbolt of the North would make a perfect wedding gift for Kyle and Katie."

Even amid the cacophony of goodbye calls and well wishes, Cole recognized the stunned silence beside him. Heresy to suggest the family's antique brooch go to the second son, he knew. But Kyle was the logical choice.

Cole had already moved out of the main house. He'd set up in the old cabin by the creek so Kyle and Katie would have some privacy. Soon their children would take over the second floor, making Kyle the patriarch of the next Erickson dynasty. And the Thunderbolt of the North was definitely a dynastic kind of possession.

As the wedding guests moved en masse toward their vehicles, Grandma finally spoke. "You're suggesting I throw away nine hundred years of tradition."

"I'm suggesting you respect nine hundred years of tradition. Kyle and Katie will have kids."

"So will you."

"Not if I don't get married."

"Of course you'll get married."

"Grandma. I'm thirty-three. Melanie was probably my best shot. Give the brooch to Katie."

"*You* are the eldest."

"Olav the Third came up with that rule in 1075. A few things have changed since then."

"The important things haven't."

"Wake up and smell the bridal bouquets. We're well into the twenty-first century. The British royal family is even talking about pushing girls up in the line of succession."

"We're not the British royal family."

"Well, thank God for that. I'd hate to have the crown jewels on my conscience."

Grandma rolled her eyes at his irreverence. She started down the stairs, and Cole automatically offered his arm and matched his pace to hers.

She gripped his elbow with a blue-veined hand. "Just because you're too lazy to find a bride—"

"Lazy?"

She tipped her chin to stare up at him. "Yes, Cole Nathaniel Walker Erickson. Lazy."

Cole tried not to smile at the ridiculous accusation. "All the more reason not to trust me with the family treasure."

"All the more reason to use a cattle prod."

He pulled back. "Ouch. Grandma, I'm shocked."

"Shocked? Oh, that you will be. Several thousand volts if you don't get your hindquarters out there and find another bride." Then her expression softened and she reached up to pat his cheek. "You're my grandson, and I love you dearly, but somebody has to make you face up to your weaknesses."

"I'm a hopeless case, Grandma," he told her honestly.

"People can change."

Cole stopped next to his pickup and swung the passenger door open. He stared into her ageless, blue eyes. "Not me."

"Why not?"

He hesitated. But if he wanted her support, he knew he had to be honest. "I make them cry, Grandma."

"That's because you leave them."

"They leave me."

She shook her head, giving him a wry half smile. "You leave them emotionally. Then they leave you physically."

"I can't change that."

"Yes you can."

Cole took a deep breath. "Give Kyle the brooch. It's the right decision."

"Find another bride. That's the right decision. You'll thank me in the end."

"Marital bliss?"

"Marital bliss."

Cole couldn't help but grin at that one. "This from a woman who once threw her husband's clothes out a second-story window."

Grandma turned away quickly, but not before he caught a glimpse of her smile.

"You know perfectly well that story is a shameless exaggeration," she said.

His grin grew. "But you admit there were men's suits scattered all over the lawn."

"I admit no such thing, Cole Nathaniel." She sniffed. "Impudent."

"Always."

"You get that from your mother. May she rest in peace."

Cole helped Grandma into the cab of the truck. "The Thunderbolt would make a perfect wedding gift."

"It will," Grandma agreed, and he felt a glimmer of hope.

Then she adjusted the hem of her dress over her knees. "You just have to find yourself a bride."

So much for hope. "Not going to happen," he said.

"You need some help?"

Cole's brain froze for a split-second, then it sputtered back to life. "Grandma…"

She folded her hands in her lap and her smile turned complacent. "We're late for the reception."

"Don't you dare."

She turned to him and blinked. "Dare what?"

"Don't you try to match me up."

"With whom?"

"Grandma."

"Close the door, dear. We're running late."

Cole opened his mouth to speak, but then snapped it shut again.

His grandmother had inherited the stubbornness and tenacity of her ancestors. He knew all about that, because he'd inherited it, too.

He banged the door shut, cursing under his breath as he rounded the front grill. There was no point in arguing anymore today. But if she started a parade of Wichita Falls' fairest and finest through the ranch house, he was going bull riding in Canada.

Cultural Properties Curator Sydney Wainsbrook felt her stomach clench and her adrenaline level rise as Bradley Slander sauntered across the foyer of New York's Laurent Museum. A champagne flute dangled carelessly from his fingers and that scheming smile made his beady brown eyes look even smaller and more ratlike than usual.

"Better luck next time, Wainsbrook," he drawled, tipping his head back to take an inelegant swig of the '96 Cristal champagne. His Adam's apple bobbed and he smacked his lips with exaggerated self-satisfaction.

Yeah, he would feel self-satisfied. He had just outbid her on an antique, gold Korean windbell, earning a hefty commission and making it the possession of a private collector instead of a public museum.

It was the third time this year he'd squatted in the wings like a vulture while she did the legwork. The third time he scrabbled in at the last second to ruin her deal.

Sydney had nothing against competition. And she understood an owner's right to sell their property to the highest bidder. What galled her was the way Bradley slithered around her contacts, fed them inflated estimates to convince them to consider auction. Then he bid much lower than his estimate, disappointing the owner and keeping important heritage finds from the community forever.

"How *do* you sleep at night?" she asked.

Bradley leaned his shoulder against a marble pillar and crossed one ankle over the other. "Let's see. I spend an hour or so in my hot tub, sip a glass of Napoleon brandy, listen to a bit of classical jazz, then crawl into my California king and close my eyes. How about you?"

She pointedly shifted her gaze to the stone wall beside them. "I fantasize about you and that broad ax."

He smirked. "Happy to be in your fantasy, babe."

"Yeah? The broad ax wins. You lose."

"Might be worth it."

"Gag me."

His lips curved up into a wider smile. "Whatever turns your crank."

A shudder ran through Sydney at the unbidden visual. She took a quick drink of her own champagne, wishing it was a good, stiff single malt. It might have been a long dry spell, but she wouldn't entertain sexual thoughts about Bradley if he was the last man on earth.

Bradley chuckled. "So, tell me. What's next?"

She raised an eyebrow.

"On your list. What are we going after? I gotta tell you, Wainsbrook, you are my ticket to the big time."

"Should I just e-mail you my research notes? Save you some trouble?"

"Whatever's most convenient."

"What's most convenient is for you to stick your head in a very dark place for a very long time."

"Sydney, Sydney, Sydney." He clucked. "And here I tell all my friends you're a lady."

"It'll be a cold day in hell before I voluntarily give you any information."

He shrugged. "Suit yourself." Then he leaned in. "I have to admit. The chase kind of turns me on."

Fighting the urge to fulfill her broad-ax fantasy, Sydney clenched her jaw. What *was* she going to do now?

She was on probation at the Laurent Museum due to her lack of productivity this year. If Bradley scooped one more of her finds, she'd be out of a job altogether. Her boss had made that much clear enough after the auction this afternoon.

What she needed was some room to maneuver. She needed to get away from Bradley, maybe leave the country. Go to Mexico, or Peru, or…France. Oh! She quickly reversed the smile that started to form.

"See?" purred Bradley. "You like the game, too. You know you do."

Sydney struggled not to gag on that one.

He held up his empty glass in a mock salute. "Until next time."

"Next time," Sydney muttered, having no intention whatsoever of giving him a next time. She figured the odds of Bradley following her overseas were remote, which meant the Thunderbolt of the North was wide open.

She had three years' worth of research notes on the legendary antique brooch, including credible evidence it was once blessed by Pope Urban the Fifth.

Forged by the Viking King, Olav the Third, in 1075, the jewel-encrusted treasure had journeyed into battles and crossed seas. Some claimed it was used as collateral to found the Sisters of Beneficence convent at La Roche.

Most thought it was a legend, but Sydney knew it existed. In somebody's attic. In somebody's jewel case. In somebody's safe-deposit box. If even half the stories were true, the Thunderbolt had an uncanny knack for survival.

And if it had survived, she'd pick up its trail. If she picked up its trail, she'd find it. And when she found it, she'd make *sure* it stayed with the Laurent Museum—even if she had to hog-tie Bradley Slander to keep him out of the bidding.

Life was looking up for Cole. He'd spent the past three days at a livestock auction in Butte, Montana, with his eye on one beauty of a quarter horse. In the end, he'd outbid outfits from California and Nevada to bring Night-Dreams home to the Valley.

He might not be in a position to produce the next round of Erickson heirs, but he was sure in a position to produce top-quality cutting horses. That had to count for something.

Cole tossed his duffel bag on the cabin floor and kicked the door shut behind him. Of course it counted for something. It counted for a lot. And he had to get his grandmother's voice out of his head.

It had been months since the wedding. He wasn't a stud, and she could only make him feel guilty if he let her.

He pulled a battered percolator from a kitchen shelf and scooped some coffee into the basket. As soon as Katie was pregnant, he'd make his case for the Thunderbolt again. If Olav the Third could start a tradition, Cole the First could change it.

He filled the coffeepot with water and cranked the knob on his propane stove. The striker clicked in the silent kitchen. Then the blue flame burst to life.

A four-cylinder engine whined its way down his dirt driveway, and Cole abandoned the coffeepot to peer out the window. His family drove eight-cylinder pickups. In fact everybody in the valley drove pickups.

He leaned over the plaid couch and watched the little sports car bump to a halt beneath his oak tree.

He didn't recognize the car. But then a trim ankle and a shapely calf stretched out the driver's door and he no longer cared.

He moved onto the porch as a telltale hiss of steam shot out from under the hood and a spurt of water dribbled down the grill. The engine gurgled a couple of times, then sighed to silence.

Another shapely leg followed the first. And a sexy pair of cream heels planted themselves in the dust.

The slim woman rose to about five-foot-five. She wore a narrow, ivory-colored skirt and a matching jacket. Thick, auburn hair cascaded over her shoulders in shimmering waves. Her cheeks were flushed and her skin was flawless. She hadn't even been in the valley long enough to get dusty.

She smiled as she turned, flashing straight white teeth and propping her sunglasses in her hair. Cole sucked in an involuntary breath.

"Hello." She waved, stumbled on the uneven ground, then quickly righted herself as she started toward him.

He trotted down the three steps to offer his arm.

"Thank you," she breathed as her slim fingers tightened against his bare forearm.

A jolt of lightning flashed all the way to his shoulder and he quickly cleared his throat. "Car trouble?" he asked.

She turned to look at the vehicle, frowning. "I don't think so."

He raised a brow. "You don't?"

She blinked up at him with jewel-green eyes. "Why would I? It seemed fine on the way in."

He stared into those eyes, trying to decide if she was wearing colored contacts. No. He didn't think so. The eyes were all hers. As was that luscious hair and those full, dark lips.

"I think you've overheated," he said, breathing heavily. He knew he sure had.

She gazed up at him in silence and her manicured nails pressed against him for a split second. "You, uh, know about cars?"

He pulled himself up a fraction of an inch. "Some."

"That's good," she said, her gaze never leaving his, the tip of her tongue flicking over her bottom lip for the barest of moments. "I mostly use taxis."

"I take it you're not from around here?" Stupid question. If she lived anywhere near Blue Earth Valley, Cole would have spotted her before now.

"New York," she said.

"The city?"

She laughed lightly and Cole's heart rate notched up. "Yes. The city."

They reached the porch and a loud spattering hiss came through the open door. The coffee. "Damn."

"What?"

"Hang on." He took the stairs in two bounds, strode across the kitchen and grabbed the handle of the coffeepot, moving it back on the stove as he shut it down.

"You burned the coffee?" she asked from behind him.

"Afraid so." He wiped up the spilled coffee then rinsed and dried his hands. Then he held one out to her. "Cole Erickson."

Her smile grew to dazzling. "Sydney Wainsbrook."

She shook his hand and the jolt of electricity doubled.

"You want me to take a look at your car?" he asked, reluctantly letting her go.

"I'd rather you offered me a cup of that coffee."

"It's ruined," he warned.

She shrugged her slim shoulders. "I'm tough."

He took in her elegant frame and choked out a short laugh. "Right."

"Hey, I'm from New York."

"This is Texas."

"Try me."

Cole bit down on his lip. Nope. Not going there.

Her eyes sparkled with mischief and she shook her head. "Walked right into that one, didn't I?"

He quickly neutralized his expression. "Walked right into what?"

She brushed past him and retrieved two stoneware mugs from the open shelf. "Don't you worry about my delicate sensibilities." She held them both out. "Pour me some coffee."

"Yes, ma'am."

Sydney ran her fingertip around the rim of the ivory coffee cup. Even by New York standards, the brew was terrible. But she was drinking every last drop. Black.

She needed Cole to know she meant business, because he looked like the kind of guy who'd walk right over her if she so much as blinked.

She contemplated him from across the table. He was a big man, all muscle and sinew beneath a worn, plaid shirt. His sleeves were rolled up, revealing tight, corded forearms. He had thick hair, a square chin, a slightly bumped nose and expressive cobalt eyes that turned sensual and made her catch her breath.

He was going to be a challenge. But then, anything to do with the Thunderbolt of the North had to be a challenge. She'd have been disappointed if it had gone any other way.

"So what brings you to Blue Earth Valley, Sydney Wainsbrook?" he drawled into the silence.

She smiled, liking her audacious plan better by the second. She'd worried he might be obnoxious or objectionable, but he was a midnight fantasy come to life. Why some other woman hadn't snapped him up before now was a mystery to her.

"You do," she said.

"Me?"

She took a sip of her coffee. "Yes, you."

"Have we met?"

"Not until now."

He sat back, blue eyes narrowing. Then a flash of comprehension crossed his face and he held up his palms. "Whoa. Wait a minute."

"What?" Surely he couldn't have figured out her plan that quickly.

"Did my grandmother put you up to this?"

Sydney shook her head, relieved. "No, she didn't."

"You sure? Because—"

"I'm sure." The only person who had put Sydney up to this was Sydney. Well, Sydney and a thousand hours of research in museum basements across Europe.

She moved her cup to one side and leaned forward, her interest piqued. "But tell me why your grandmother might have sent me."

He tightened his jaw and sat back in purposeful silence.

Sydney wriggled a little in her seat. "Hoo-ha. I can tell this is going to be good."

He didn't answer, just stared her down.

"Dish," she insisted, refusing to be intimidated. She had a feeling people normally gave him a wide berth. And she had no intention of behaving like normal people. Surprise was one of her best weapons.

He rolled his eyes. "Fine. It's because she's an incorrigible matchmaker."

Sydney bit down on a laugh. "Your grandmother is setting you up?"

He grimaced. "That sounded pathetic, didn't it?"

"A little."

"She's a meddler. And…well…" He seemed to catch himself, and he quickly shook his head. "Nah. Not going there. You tell me what you're doing in Blue Earth Valley."

Sydney wrapped her hands around her coffee cup. Right. Stalling wasn't going to change a thing. She'd plunge right in and hope to catch him off guard. "I'm a curator from the Laurent Museum."

He didn't react. Didn't show any signs of panic. That was good.

"I've just finished three months' research in Europe."

He waited. Still no reaction.

"It supplemented three years of previous research. My thesis, actually."

"You wrote a thesis?"

"Yes, I did. On the Thunderbolt of the North."

Okay. That got a reaction from him. His eyes chilled to sea ice and his jaw clamped tight.

"I understand you're the current owner."

His palms came down hard on the table. "You understand wrong."

"Let me rephrase—"

"Good idea."

She leaned in again. "I know how it works."

"You know how *what* works?"

"The inheritance. I know it goes to your wife. And I'm here to offer to marry you."

Two

Everything inside Cole stilled.

He opened his mouth, then he snapped it shut again.

He stared at the perfectly gorgeous creature in front of him and tried to make sense out the situation. Was this a joke?

"Did Kyle put you up to this?" he asked.

"Who's Kyle?"

"My brother."

She shook her head and all that auburn hair fanned out around her perfectly made-up face. "It wasn't your brother, and it wasn't your grandmother."

"Then who?"

"Me."

He paused again. "You seriously expect me to believe you came all the way from New York—"

"Yes, I do." She reached into her clutch purse and pulled out a business card.

He read it. Sure enough, Laurent Museum. Okay, now he was just getting annoyed. The Thunderbolt wasn't a commodity to be bartered. It was a trust, a duty. "So was that breakdown nothing but a setup?"

"What breakdown?"

"Your car."

"My car is fine."

"Your car is fried."

"You know, I just proposed to you."

He stood up. "And you thought I'd say yes?"

"I'd hoped—"

"In what universe?" His voice rose, bouncing off the cabin walls. He was offended, offended on behalf of his grandmother, his ancestors and his heirs. "In what *universe* would I agree to marry a complete stranger and give away a family heirloom?"

She stood, too. "Oh, no. I didn't mean—"

"I have horses to shoe." He was done listening. She could fix her own car for all he cared, or call a taxi or hoof it up to the main road.

"Right now?" she asked.

"Right now." He scooped a battered Stetson from a hook on the wall and stuffed it on his head.

Sydney watched Cole march out of the small log cabin. Okay, that hadn't gone quite as well as she'd hoped. But then again, he hadn't really given her a chance to explain. She wasn't trying to *steal* the Thunderbolt. She merely wanted to display it for a few months.

She was pulling together a Viking show exceptional enough for front gallery space at the Laurent. With the Thunderbolt as the centerpiece, she would thwart Bradley

Slander and save her career. All she needed was the cooperation of one cowboy.

She moved to the cabin door and watched him head up a rise while she contemplated her next move.

The man had the broadest shoulders she'd ever seen. Solid as an oak tree, he had a confident stride and a butt that could stop traffic. She watched for a few more steps, then she forced her gaze away. His butt was irrelevant. The marriage would be in name only.

Her focus had to be on the brooch, not on the man. It wasn't as if she could put Cole on display in the front gallery. Although…

She squelched a grin and glanced at the rental car.

A breakdown, huh? Car trouble could be her ticket to more time with him. Swallowing the dregs of her coffee, she made up her mind. If that baby wasn't broken down now, it soon would be.

She waited until Cole disappeared over the hill. Then she popped the hood, yanked out some random wires and closed it up again, hoping she'd done some serious damage.

Dusting off her hands, she tucked her clutch purse under her arm and headed up the hill.

Three-inch heels were definitely not the best choice for the Erickson Ranch. Neither was a straight skirt and loose hair. By the time she closed in on Cole, she was disheveled and out of breath. She'd scratched her hand ducking through a barbed-wire fence, got a cactus stuck to the toe of her shoe and attracted a pair of horseflies that were now moving in for the kill.

Cole looked completely unfazed by the climb. He stood a hundred yards away, on the crest of the hill, with a coiled rope in one hand. He raised his thumb and index finger to his mouth and let out a shrill whistle that she was willing to bet would get the attention of every cab driver on Fifth Avenue.

The ground rumbled beneath her feet and she took an involuntary step backward. Then she forced herself to hold still and sucked in a bracing breath. If it was a stampede, it was a stampede.

The Thunderbolt had the power to launch her career to the stratosphere. And she'd studied too long and too hard to quit now. Better to be trampled to death trying to get her hands on it than give up and become a tour guide.

A herd of some twenty horses appeared on the ridge, their manes and tails flowing in a wave of black, brown and silver. In the face of their onslaught, Cole stood his ground. He lifted his battered cowboy hat and waved it in the air. The herd slowed, parted around him, then shuffled to a stop.

Okay. Now *that* was sexy.

And she wasn't dead.

The day was looking up.

Cole captured a big gray horse and led it through a gate. Sydney quickly followed. She was intimidated by the big animal, but she was more frightened of the two dozen of his friends they were leaving behind.

Cole tied up the horse then ran his hands soothingly along its neck. "Was there something about my *no* that was ambiguous?" he asked Sydney.

She found a log to perch on and gingerly plucked at the little round cactus on her shoe. Her skirt would probably be ruined, but that couldn't be helped. She played dumb. "You said no?"

He turned to stare at her for a moment. "Just in case you missed it the first time, no."

"You haven't heard me out."

"You're trying to steal my family heirloom. What's to

hear out?" With a firm pat on the horse's neck, he headed for a nearby shack.

She scrambled to her feet and followed. "I wasn't going to keep the brooch."

He opened the door. "Ah. Well, in that case..."

Her spirits rose. "Yes?"

"No." His answer was flat as he retrieved a wooden box and a battered metal stand.

Once again, he hadn't let her give enough information for a logical decision. "Are you always this unreasonable?"

"Yes."

"You are not."

He pulled the door shut. "Are you always this stubborn?"

"Will you at least listen to my offer?"

"No."

"Why not?"

"Have *you* ever listened to the wedding vows?"

"Of course."

He started back to the horse. "There's a little thing in there about loving and honoring and till death do us part. And there's generally a preacher standing in front of you, along with your family and friends when you make those promises."

Sydney hesitated. She hadn't actually thought through the details of the ceremony. She'd pictured something in a courthouse, a minimum number of words, mail-order wedding bands and a chaste kiss at the end.

"I could honor you," she offered.

He stopped and turned, leaning slightly forward to pin her with a midnight-blue stare. "Could you love me?"

Sydney stilled. What kind of a question was that?

His gaze bore into hers, searching deep, as if sifting through her hopes and fears.

She knew how to love. She'd loved her foster parents. She loved her mother. But those loves turned bittersweet when her parents died in the house fire and her aging foster parents passed away five years ago.

"Hey there, Cole," came a laughing feminine voice.

Sydney quickly pulled back, shaking off the unsettling memories.

Cole focused his attention over her shoulder.

"Hey, Katie." He nodded.

"You been holding out on us?" asked the voice.

Sydney turned to see a woman on horseback come to a stop in front of the little shed. She had shoulder-length brown hair tied back in a ponytail. A cowboy hat dangled between her shoulder blades, and her burgundy shirt and crisp blue jeans made her look as if she had ridden out of a Western movie.

Her saddle leather creaked as she dismounted.

"What?" asked Cole. "You wanted to shoe the horses?"

The woman smirked as she led her chestnut horse forward. Then her smile turned friendly and she stretched her hand out to Sydney. "Katie Erickson. Cole's sister-in-law."

Sydney reached out to shake the woman's surprisingly strong hand. "Sydney Wainsbrook."

"Nice to meet you," said Katie. She glanced speculatively at Cole for a split second before returning her attention to Sydney. "And what brings you to Blue Earth Valley?"

Sydney took in Cole's determined expression and decided she had little to lose. "I'm here to marry Cole."

He sputtered an inarticulate sound.

But Katie shrieked in delight and her horse startled. "So you *were* holding out on us."

"She's only after the Thunderbolt," said Cole, planting the metal stand with disgust.

But Katie's attention was all on Sydney. "How long have you known him? Where did you meet?" Her gaze strayed to Sydney's bare fingers. "Did he propose yet?"

"I proposed to him."

"She's after the Thunderbolt," Cole repeated. "She's a con artist."

"I'm a museum curator. I want to display the Thunderbolt. But I really am willing to marry him."

"She's—" Cole threw up his hands, turning to pace back to the horse. "Forget it."

Katie called after him. "Don't be so hasty, Cole. It sounds like a good offer. And you're not getting any younger, you know."

He muttered something unintelligible.

Katie laughed, turning back to Sydney. "From a museum, you say?"

"The Laurent."

"In New York?"

"Yes."

Katie's reaction to the proposition wasn't nearly as negative as Cole's. Maybe she would listen to reason. Maybe she would even have some influence over her brother-in-law.

"I was planning to display the Thunderbolt temporarily," said Sydney, keeping her voice loud enough to be sure Cole would hear. "It would only be a loan."

"How did you know it went to his wife?" asked Katie.

"Research."

"And how did you know he wasn't already married?"

"More research." Sydney raised her voice again. "I was thinking of something simple and temporary. At the courthouse."

"A marriage of convenience," Katie nodded.

"Right."

"And how would that be convenient for me?" Cole's hammer came down on a metal horseshoe and the rhythmic clanks echoed through the pasture.

"You could think of it as a public service," said Sydney.

"I'm not altruistic."

"You'd bring an important antiquity to the attention of the world."

"It's a private possession."

"It would only be a loan."

"Why don't you give up?"

While Sydney formulated a response, Katie spoke up. "Why don't you come for dinner instead?"

"*Katie,*" Cole stressed, wiping the sweat from his brow.

"We can talk about it, Cole," said Katie. "No harm in talking about it."

Sydney felt a surge of hope. She definitely had an ally in Katie.

"You two can do whatever you want," said Cole, going back to hammering. "But I'm not coming to dinner."

"Of course you are," said Katie.

"Nope."

"I'll send Kyle after you."

"Good luck with that."

Katie put her hands on her hips and arched one eyebrow.

"You really need to do something about your wife," said Cole as he leaned on the rail next to the barbecue where his brother was grilling steaks.

Kyle closed the cast-iron lid and joined Cole. "It's not my fault you can't say no to her."

"Can *you* say no to her?"

"Why would I want to say no to her?"

"Not ever?"

"Not ever."

Cole folded his arms over his chest. "Don't you ever need to just put your foot down and lay out the logic?"

Kyle laughed. "You're joking, right?"

"How can a man live with somebody orchestrating his every move?"

"Are we talking about Katie or Sydney?"

"Katie's helping Sydney. And we're talking about women in general."

"And your fear of them."

"Don't be absurd."

"Then why are you freaking out over Sydney's idea?"

Cole peered at his brother, squinting in the dying light of the sunset. "Are you seriously suggesting I marry a stranger and give her the Thunderbolt?"

"She's from a museum, not some crime family. I'm only suggesting you hear her out."

Katie appeared in the doorway, a big wooden salad bowl clasped in her hands. "Hear who out?"

"Sydney," said Kyle.

"Oh, good," said Katie. "We're just in time."

Sydney appeared behind her with a basket of rolls, and Cole did an involuntary double take. She'd removed her jacket and her silk, butter-yellow blouse highlighted the halo of her rich, auburn hair. Her rounded breasts pressed against the thin fabric, and a small flash of her stomach peeked out between the hem of her blouse and the waistband of her skirt.

"Can you open the wine?" Katie asked Cole.

"Uh, sure," said Cole, with a mental shake, telling himself to quit acting like a teenager. He reached for the corkscrew.

"I was the high bid on Night-Dreams," he said to his

brother, not so subtly changing the direction of the conversation.

Kyle shot him a knowing grin but played along. "Planning to use Sylvester as a sire?"

Cole popped the cork on the bottle of merlot. "Come next spring, it's the start of a whole new bloodline."

After Sydney set the rolls down on the table, Cole automatically pulled out her chair. She accepted with a smile of thanks, and the scent of her perfume wafted under his nose.

"That reminds me," said Kyle from the other side of the table. "I need your signature on a contract with Everwood." He transferred the sizzling steaks from the grill to a wooden platter. "Gave me my price. He'll take all the beef we can supply."

Cole masked a spurt of frustration by focusing on the wine-pouring. He hated that Kyle had to run to him for every little signature. His brother was an incredibly talented cattleman, and the tradition that put the ranch solely in the name of the eldest son was archaic and unfair.

"Way to go," he said to Kyle, setting out the glasses. "You always were the brains of the outfit."

Kyle scoffed. "Yeah, right."

Cole pulled out his own chair and held up his glass in a toast to his brother's advantageous deal. "I'm dead serious about that."

"Are we going to talk shop all night?" asked Katie, sitting down.

Simultaneously, Cole said yes while Kyle said no. They both sat down.

Sydney leaned forward. "Maybe we could talk about my shop."

"I'm deeding you half the ranch," Cole said to Kyle, without so much as glancing in Sydney's direction.

Those words had the effect he was looking for. The air went flat-dead silent. The barbecue hissed once, and a sparrow chirped from the poplar trees.

"I talked to a tax lawyer in Dallas last week," Cole continued, reaching for a roll. "About our options."

"Cole," Kyle cautioned.

"I figure we can subdivide along Spruce Ridge, then follow the creek bed to the road."

Kyle planted the butt of his steak knife on the wooden table. "Stop."

"I'm going to do it," said Cole.

"Oh, no, you're not."

"You can't stop me."

"Boys," Katie interrupted.

"Oh, yes, I can," said Kyle. "I won't accept."

"It's not up to you." Cole took a breath. The guilt on this one had been burning inside him for a long time. He wasn't about to back off. "Sometimes a man has to put his foot down and make decisions that are in the best interest of his family."

"Was that a slam?" asked Kyle.

"No."

"It sounded like a slam."

Cole dropped the roll to his plate, regretting his choice of words. "I didn't mean that. I meant, a man needs his own land."

"Kyle?" Katie tried again. "Cole?"

"You saying all these years I haven't had my own land."

That threw Cole. "Of course not."

"There you go."

"What about your kids?"

Kyle clenched his jaw but remained silent.

Cole hoped that meant his brother was running low on

arguments. "You need to build a legacy for your kids." He rushed on. "You need to leave them something. If you won't think of yourself, think about your children."

Sydney's hand touched Cole's thigh. His muscle immediately convulsed and he shot her a stunned look.

"Let's move on," said Kyle, a steely thread to his voice.

Cole looked back at his brother. "Let's agree to go to Dallas and talk to the lawyers."

Sydney's fingernails tightened, jolting Cole's nervous system.

What the hell was she doing?

"It's not just you anymore," Cole said to Kyle. "You have a family—"

Sydney pinched him. It actually hurt.

He swung his gaze back to her, but caught Katie's expression on the way.

He stopped.

He stared at his sister-in-law's white lips. "Katie?"

Kyle pulled back his chair as Katie started to tremble.

Katie stood and Kyle rose with her.

"What?" Cole jumped up. "What's wrong?"

Katie gave a little shake of her head and waved away their concern. "I'm fine."

"You're not fine," said Cole.

She placed her hand on Kyle's arm. "I'm really okay. I'm just going to get a glass of water."

Kyle put an arm around her shoulders and gave her a little squeeze. "You sure?" he whispered.

She nodded. "Really. The less fuss, the better. I'll be right back."

Kyle watched her disappear into the kitchen.

Cole raked a hand through his hair, trying to sift through the turn of events. "I'm sorry," he said. "What the heck..."

"Can I help?" Sydney asked Kyle.

Kyle closed his eyed and dropped back into his chair. He shook his head. "It's the talk of kids."

Cole slowly sat, opening his mouth to ask for an explanation, but Sydney's fingers closed on his thigh again.

He felt like a bull in a china shop. What was he missing here?

"She hoped to be pregnant by now," said Kyle.

Cole went cold.

Sydney tossed her napkin onto the table. "I am going to make sure she's okay."

Both men rose with her.

After Sydney disappeared, Kyle moved restlessly to the rail, taking a long, steady swig of his wine.

Cole followed, not sure of what to say. He and Kyle didn't exactly have heart-to-heart talks about their sex lives, never mind their sperm counts. Was this a medical problem? Did they need to see a doctor?

"Are you..." he began. "Uh, do you..."

"The doctor thinks it's stress," said Kyle. "But we don't know anything for sure, and Katie's worried she'll never have kids."

Cole could have kicked himself. "And I was a big help."

Kyle snorted out a dry chuckle as he gazed out over the Blue Hills. "Next time, watch my expression and grab a clue."

"Next time I'll pay attention when Sydney mangles my thigh." Cole regretted his bull-headed stupidity. "Is there anything I can do to help?"

"Get married and have some babies so Katie doesn't have this whole dynasty thing on her shoulders."

"That would be a trick."

"Hey, you've got a bona fide offer in my kitchen."

"We could have a bona fide con artist in your kitchen.

Besides, Sydney doesn't want babies, she wants the Thunderbolt. I'm pretty sure this is a platonic offer."

Kyle turned to face Cole. He braced his elbow on the rail and a speculative gleam rose in his eyes.

"What?" asked Cole, dragging the word out slowly, trepidation rising.

"You wouldn't *really* have to have babies with Sydney," said Kyle. "You'd just have to let Katie *think* you'll have babies with Sydney."

"That's insane." And even if it wasn't, Katie knew why Sydney was here. There's no way they'd ever convince her they were having babies together.

"No." Kyle shook his head. "It's brilliant. You pretend to fall in love with her, pretend to marry her for real. She gets the brooch and Katie relaxes enough to get pregnant."

"And I get a wife I don't know, who doesn't love me, won't sleep with me but takes my jewelry?"

Kyle took another swig of his wine. "I'm sure you're not the first guy that's happened to."

Cole snorted.

Kyle clapped him on the shoulder. "You get the satisfaction of knowing you put your foot down and made a decision that was best for your family."

"Somehow I don't think this is me putting my foot down."

"So you'll do it?"

"I never said that." How could Cole justify getting married on the off chance it would help Katie get pregnant? Then again, how could he justify not getting married if there was a chance it could help Katie get pregnant?

"We'd be lying to your wife," he pointed out to Kyle, looking for some loophole that didn't make him the bad guy.

"No, we wouldn't. We wouldn't have to say a thing. Katie's a hopeless romantic. Trust me, she's going to throw you and Sydney together no matter what you and I decide. All you'd have to do is hang around and look besotted."

"I don't do besotted."

"Just look at Sydney the way you were looking at her before dinner."

"I haven't—"

"That was more aroused than besotted, I'll admit. But it should work."

"You're out of your mind."

"She's a babe, Cole. It's not like it would be this huge hardship."

Alarm crept into Cole's system as Kyle's words started to make some kind of bizarre sense. He couldn't consider this. Then again, he couldn't *not* consider this.

"This is the dumbest plan I've ever heard," he said. "Take Katie on a vacation. She can relax on the beach. I'll pay."

"She'll worry about you."

"She doesn't have to worry about me."

"I know that, and you know that, but Katie…"

It was Cole's turn to gaze at the dark hillsides across the lake. "You know, this morning things were looking pretty good for me. I'd just bought a new mare. I was minding my own business, thinking about shoeing, thinking about building a new hay shed, maybe buying a combine…"

Kyle started to laugh.

"Then along comes Sydney Wainsbrook and suddenly she's taking over my life."

"Kyle?" Katie called from the kitchen.

"Yes, sweetheart?" he called back.

"Do you think it's too late for Sydney to drive to Wichita Falls all by herself?"

"Of course it's too late." Kyle waggled a victorious eyebrow at Cole. "It's way too late."

"She's going to stay over," Katie called.

"Sounds good."

"I haven't agreed to anything," Cole muttered to his brother.

"You have the easy part," said Kyle. "Just hang around and look besotted."

"I'm going home."

"Come back for breakfast."

"Nope."

"I'll send Katie after you."

"Good luck with that."

Three

Cole was steadfastly chowing down on hotcakes and coffee when a knock came on his cabin door.

"Come in," he called gruffly, ready to take on Kyle or Katie or both.

But it was Sydney who poked her head around the door. "Hey, Cole."

Cole cringed, cussing inside his head. *Low blow, Kyle.* "Good morning, Sydney."

She gestured inside. "May I?"

No, never. "Of course."

Her lips curved into that brilliant, sexy smile. "Thanks," she breathed, messing with both his equilibrium and his libido.

Katie had obviously lent her some clothes. Instead of her impractical suit, Sydney wore a tight pair of faded blue jeans, a short T-shirt, and her hair was pulled back in a perky ponytail. Her makeup was more subtle than yesterday but, if anything, it made her sexier.

"Coffee?" he asked, finding his voice and rising from his chair.

"Love some."

"It's a little better than yesterday." One cup of coffee. That was it. And no matter what, he wasn't letting her talk him into going back to the house for breakfast.

Kyle's plan might be crazy, but Cole knew he'd cave—even if there was only a slight chance it would help Katie get pregnant. Because Katie without babies was positively unthinkable. She'd be the greatest mother in the world.

"Yesterday's coffee was fine," said Sydney.

"You lie," said Cole.

She shrugged. "I've had worse."

"Don't know where." He put a fresh, steaming mug on the table in front of her.

"Sherman's on West Fifty-second. Ever been to New York?"

"Never have. You hungry?"

"Katie made eggs."

He nodded and sat back down. "How's she doing?"

Sydney wrapped her hands around the mug. "Sad, I think."

Cole nodded, trying not to feel like a heel.

"You know your brother's come up with a plan to fix this, right?" she asked.

Every muscle in Cole's body contracted. His brother had brought Sydney into the loop? Why, that low-down, sneaky…

He bought a few seconds by taking a swallow of his coffee. "What kind of a plan?"

"He said he'd explained it all to you last night."

Of course he did. "What did he tell you?"

"That my timing couldn't have been better. That you and I should get married and let Katie think we're expanding the Erickson dynasty."

It was a conspiracy. It was a bloody conspiracy. "You actually think Katie will fall for it?"

Sydney gazed knowingly at him from under her thick lashes. "You don't think she'll believe you're interested in me?"

"Fishing?"

Her smile turned self-conscious and she gave a shrug. "Maybe."

"Or cornering me, perhaps?"

Her smiled widened then. "Maybe that, too."

Cole sighed. "I meant no disrespect to you." He simply didn't want to marry a stranger. Was that such a horrible thing?

Sydney was assessing him with those gorgeous green eyes. "Okay, I'll go first. You're a good-looking, sexy guy. It's not a big stretch for Katie to think I might go for you."

Cole's chest tightened on the word sexy.

It was Sydney who wrote the book on sexy. The way she moved with such fluid grace. The way her husky voice caught on that trembling laugh.

He could still feel her touch on his arm, on his thigh. Okay, so the thigh one wasn't the most pleasant memory in the world. But it was still sexy. Which was pretty pathetic.

"Cole?"

"Hmm?"

"I think it's a good plan."

"Of course you do."

"If we're lucky, it'll help Katie. It'll definitely help the

Laurent—a respected public institution, I might point out. So where's the harm?"

"Don't you have places to go? Things to dig up?"

"That's archeologists. There's nothing higher on my priority list than the Thunderbolt."

Cole pushed aside his pancakes.

She wanted to take this seriously? Okay. They'd take it seriously for a minute. "What about your family? You'd lie to them about getting married?"

She waved a hand. "Not an issue."

"You're not close to them?" That surprised Cole. She was such a smart, perky, good-natured woman. What kind of a family wouldn't want to stay close to her?

A shadow crossed her face. "My foster parents died five years ago."

Cole's stomach clenched in sympathy. He knew what it was like to lose parents. "I'm sorry to hear that."

She shook her head. "It's okay."

"What about brothers and sisters?"

"None."

His sympathy rush escalated. Now he had a sexy, vulnerable little orphan Annie challenging him to do right by his sister-in-law.

He stood up and took his dishes to the sink.

She followed. "Cole?"

"Yeah." And there was that elusive scent again. He didn't dare turn around.

"Why are you hesitating? We can draft whatever legal documents you want to protect the Thunderbolt."

"It's not that." Well, actually, it was that. At least, that was part of it. He didn't know Sydney, and he'd be a fool to trust her.

But there was more to it than the legal risks. It was a

marriage, a marriage to a woman he didn't love, didn't even know. Maybe he was an old-fashioned guy, but he just couldn't bring himself to do it.

"The Laurent is a very reputable institution," she said.

"I believe you."

"Is it lying to Katie, then?"

Cole turned. And there was Sydney, mere inches away. A slight movement of his hand and he'd be touching her. A tip of his head and he'd be kissing her.

"It's lying to Katie," he said. "Lying to Grandma. Lying to God."

"We could have a civil service."

"Not a possibility."

She tipped her head, looking perplexed.

He moved in, just a little, pressing his point, hoping he could make her understand and give up on this ridiculous idea. "We're talking about my family here, and they know me very well. They know that if I loved someone—if I *truly* loved someone—I sure wouldn't say so in a civic office in front of a clerk and two impartial witnesses."

Sydney bit down on her bottom lip. Her cat-green eyes narrowed in concentration, but she didn't respond.

"You ready to walk down the aisle in a white dress, promise to love me and honor me, then kiss me and throw a bouquet?"

As he outlined the scenario, an unexpected vision bloomed in Cole's mind. Sydney in a white dress. Sydney in a veil. Sydney with a spray of delicate roses trembling in her hands. He could feel her skin, smell her perfume, taste the sweetness of her lush lips.

"We'd both know it was fake," she said.

Cole startled out of the vision and gave a short nod. "Yeah. Right. We'd both know it was fake."

"And that's what would matter. That's what would count." She squared her shoulders. "Knowing the benefits, I could do it."

Cole clenched his jaw. He'd hand the Thunderbolt over to her tomorrow if he could. But Olav the Third was specific, and Cole's grandfather's will was ironclad.

He examined the idea from every angle. From his, from Kyle's, from Katie's, from Sydney's.

She could do it? Of course she could. It wasn't as if it would be physically painful. And nobody would die. And nobody would ever be the wiser. Marriages failed all the time. After a decent interval, he and Sydney could simply divorce.

"Then so can I," said Cole, just as he'd known he would from the second his brother conceived the plan. His family needed him, and that was an unconditional trump card.

A brilliant smile lit Sydney's face. "Where do we start?"

"First thing we have to do," said Cole two hours later while Sydney watched him saddle a horse outside his cabin, "is convince Katie I'm falling for you."

Sydney eyed up the big animal from the safety of his porch, having second and third and fourth thoughts. Oh, not about marrying Cole; she was completely convinced that was the right thing to do. She was having second thoughts about getting on the back of an animal that could crush her with one stomp of its foot.

"Tell me again why that has to involve horses?" she said.

"Don't you watch the movies?" Cole pressed his knee into the horse's ribs and pulled snug on a leather strap. His strong, calloused hands worked with practiced ease, and she had a sudden vision of them against her pale skin.

He released a stirrup and secured a buckle. "People who are falling in love gallop their horses along the beach all the time."

Maybe so. But there was no way in this world Sydney was galloping any horse anywhere anytime soon. "Couldn't we just go to a movie?"

He rocked the saddle back and forth on the horse's back. "Where?"

"I don't know."

"It's a long way to Wichita Falls."

"What about a picnic? You, me, some ants, maybe a bottle of wine?"

"We want Katie to see us."

Good point. Cole and Sydney alone in a meadow didn't do anybody any good. Well, except maybe for the cowboy Viking fantasy she was working on. The one where Cole dragged her into his strong arms and kissed her until she swooned.

"Maybe you could double me on your horse?" That ought to give Katie something to think about.

"I wouldn't do that to my horse."

"Hey!"

He rolled his eyes. "Don't be so sensitive. I'm the heavy one, not you."

She scrambled for an alternative, any alternative. "I know. We could mess up our clothes and our hair and let Katie think we had sex."

He walked the smaller of the two horses over to the porch. "On our first date?"

"What? Are you a prude?"

"No, I'm not a prude. Come over here and get on."

She shook her head, moving backward until she came up against the cabin wall. "Then why not on a first date?"

"Because I'm supposed to be falling in love with you. Come on. Clarabelle won't hurt you."

He couldn't have sex if he was falling in love? "Don't tell me this is a good girl, bad girl thing."

His eyes darkened to cobalt and a shiver ran up her spine. "This is a horseback-riding thing."

"Because, if you've got some hang-up—"

"What? You'll refuse to marry me." His look turned challenging.

But then, Sydney was up for a challenge. There was nothing wrong with sex on a first date. Not that she'd ever done it. But she could have if she'd wanted to.

"I won't refuse to marry you," she answered, striking a pose. "But you'll have to tell me which kind of girl you want me to be."

His nostrils flared.

There. Now he was the one off balance. She took a few bold steps forward and her breasts came level with his eyes.

She made a show of reaching past his shoulder to pat the horse. It twitched at the contact—a warm muscle jumping against her fingers. She let her voice go husky. "Which kind do you want me to be, Cole?"

"Sydney."

"Hmm?"

"Don't do this."

"Don't do what?"

"Don't flirt with me."

She blinked in mock innocence. "I'm simply asking a question."

"No, you're not." He swung up on the porch, positioning himself behind her, speaking very close to her right ear, making her skin vibrate with his gravelly, sensual voice. "What you're asking for is trouble."

He was right. Tall, strong, sexy and right. And if that was trouble, bring it on.

But his voice went back to normal. "Hold on to the saddle horn," he instructed, placing his hand on the back of hers and moving it into place. "You're going to put your left foot in the stirrup and swing your leg over the saddle."

Sydney tensed. Flirting, she knew. Horses were something else entirely. "Listen, I've never, ever—"

"It's easy."

She fought his grip. "Cole."

"She's calm and gentle, and she'll follow right along behind me."

"I'm scared," Sydney admitted. What if the horse bucked? What if she fell? What if she was trampled?

"Tighten your grip." He pressed her hand against the hard leather of the horn. His palm was warm and sure, and for a moment she relaxed.

"I'm right behind you." He nudged her forward, urging her closer to the horse. "Foot in the stirrup now."

She took a deep breath and did it.

"Up and over." He placed a broad palm under her butt and all but lifted her into position.

It was a quick thrill, but a thrill all the same. And now she was straddling a shifting horse, staring down at a rough-and-ready cowboy with a knowing glint in his blue eyes.

She could feel the heat coming off her cheeks and tiny quivers jumping in her thigh muscles.

"For the record," he said, back to husky and sexy.

"Yeah?"

"You should feel free to be good *and* bad."

It was a long mile from Cole's cabin near the creek up to Katie and Kyle's house on the hill. They took it at a slow walk, and Clarabelle followed the black horse along a faint trail through a wildflower meadow. Sydney's thigh muscles grew tight, but otherwise the ride went without incident.

"Katie said you used to live up here," she called to Cole as the two-story house rose up in front of them.

He twisted in the saddle to look back. "I moved out when Kyle got married."

"Was it just the two of you?"

He nodded, then did something to drop his horse back so they were side by side. "My parents died when I was twenty. Kyle was eighteen."

"I'm sorry."

"It was tough. But at least we had Grandma."

"The matchmaking grandmother."

Cole smiled. Then his eyes dimmed. "She's going to be really excited about you."

Sydney felt a twinge of guilt. Grandmas didn't seem like the kind of people you should lie to.

"Will it be okay?" she asked.

He seemed to ponder the question. "Well, she'll definitely book the church. Probably start baking the cake."

He brought the horses to a halt but didn't dismount. "You know, if we want to pull this off, we'd better make sure we have our stories straight."

Trying to lighten the mood, she tossed her hair over her shoulders. "How about you fell head over heels and I'm marrying you out of pity?"

"That'll work."

"Cole, I was only—"

"It *will* work."

Katie appeared at the back door, giving an exuberant wave. "Sydney. You're still here?"

Sydney smiled at Katie. "Cole offered to teach me how

to ride," she called back, deciding it was better to stick to the truth as far as they could.

Katie skipped toward them. "That's fantastic."

Sydney shifted in her saddle. "It's pretty hard on the butt. I don't know how you guys do it."

"Callouses," said Cole as he dismounted. Then he grinned at her. "You'll be developing some soon."

Was he flirting?

He looked as though he was flirting.

And she'd sure felt a shiver at the reference to her butt.

He walked a few paces and tied his horse. Then he came back for her. "You want some help down?"

"Sure," she said. It wasn't as if she had a hope of getting off by herself. Plus, her skin was already tingling in anticipation of his hands.

"Kick out both feet," he instructed. "We don't want you getting hung up."

She kicked free of the stirrups.

Katie grabbed the bridle and held the horse steady.

"Lean forward and bring the other leg over his back," said Cole.

She did.

Cole wrapped his hands around her waist and slowly lowered her to the ground.

It wasn't nearly as exciting as mounting the horse, but she got to inhale his scent, and for a second there his body was pressed full length against her back. She shivered deep down inside.

He didn't immediately step away.

"She's catching on pretty well," he said to Katie. Then he leaned around and brushed a lock of hair from Sydney's cheek. "She'll be running barrels in no time." He gave her shoulders a little squeeze before shifting away.

Sydney blinked at him in amazement. She'd never met anyone so caring and attentive. It was almost as if… She stopped herself. He was playacting. Wow. He was very good at it.

Katie let go of the horse's bridle and reached for Sydney's hand. "So you *are* staying for a while?"

"Okay with you?" Cole asked.

"Of course it is." Katie gave Sydney's hand a quick squeeze. "You're welcome to stay with us as long as you like."

Cole led Clarabelle to the post and tied her alongside his black horse while Katie insisted they come in.

The visit didn't last long before pillars of black clouds moved down the valley. Soon, fat raindrops plunked onto the warm earth and battered against the windows.

Kyle arrived, taking refuge from the storm, shaking his hat and wiping raindrops off his face.

Katie greeted him with a hug and a kiss, and Cole moved up close to Sydney's ear. "Okay," he whispered, glancing surreptitiously at his brother and sister-in-law. "This is perfect."

"What? You mean me?" Was she hitting just the right note here?

"No. I mean the rain."

Oh. Sydney glanced out the window. Perfect wasn't exactly the word she'd use to describe the growing torrent. "Is there a forest fire or something?"

"No. But the horses are all wet now. And so is the tack. It's going to be a miserable ride back to my place." Cole sounded unnaturally excited by the prospect.

Sydney grimaced. "Well, it doesn't get much more perfect than that, does it?" Her inner thighs chafed at the thought of getting back on a dry saddle, never mind a wet one.

He patted one of her shoulders. "You need to think strategically."

"Okay." She nodded slowly, trying to figure out how the rain fit into their plans. Would it flood the road? Maroon them together?

"When Kyle and Katie break it up back there," said Cole, "I'll suggest we ride home. Kyle will offer to ride Clarabelle, but you insist on doing it yourself."

Sydney watched the raindrops battering the window pane. "And why would I do that?" Other than a latent masochistic streak.

"You want to be with me, of course. You're dying to spend time with me, because I'm so sexy and irresistible."

Sydney cocked her head to one side. "How could I possibly forget?"

"I don't know. Thing is, if you're willing to ride a wet horse through a rainstorm, Katie will know you're in deep."

It made sense, in a wet, squishy, ugly kind of way. Sydney steeled herself. So be it. She was prepared to take one for the Thunderbolt.

"So Kyle knows about the plan?" she asked.

Cole shook his head. "I just came up with it."

"What if he doesn't offer?"

"Don't be ridiculous."

She gave him a questioning look.

"If he didn't offer, we'd have to kick him out of Texas. Now, no matter what he says, you ride that horse."

"This is secretly revenge, isn't it?"

Cole tapped the tip of her nose with his index finger. "Nah. When it's revenge, you'll know it."

Cole's plan worked like a charm.

Soon Sydney stood dripping wet and saddle sore in the middle of his cabin. And, though he was just as soaked as her, he had gallantly lit a fire then gone back outside to take care of the horses.

She'd briefly considered offering to help. But she was exhausted. Instead, she shook the droplets from her hands, finger-combed her hair and glanced around the little room.

She had to admit, the cabin was charming and homey in the rain. It was built of peeled logs that had mellowed to a golden yellow. The floor was hardwood, scattered with rugs, and the walls were decorated with antique pictures and hurricane lamps. The pieces weren't valuable, but she suspected Cole's ancestors had purchased them and handed them down over many generations.

She ran her finger along the stone fireplace mantel as she moved closer to the heat. It was only September, but there was a definite chill in the air. A plaid armchair with a folded knit blanket looked inviting. Too bad she'd soak the upholstery.

Cole returned, banging the door shut behind him.

"You should go get dry," he said as he pulled off his dripping Stetson and hung it on a peg. "There are a couple of robes on the back of the bathroom door. I'll make us a hot drink."

"I should do something to help." Not that she didn't appreciate this gallant he-man stuff. But she was beginning to feel like a dead weight.

He shook off the sleeves of his denim shirt. "Don't worry about it."

But she did worry about it. He'd agreed to marry her, and she didn't want him to change his mind because he thought she was high maintenance. "Am I keeping you from work?"

He jerked his thumb toward the kitchen window. "In *that?* Are you going to be a nagging wife?"

Sydney couldn't help but smile. "Sorry."

"Get dried off. I can't marry you if you've got pneumonia."

She gave up. She left Cole to the teakettle and closeted herself in the tiny bathroom, stripping off her wet clothes. There was barely room to turn around in there. She banged her butt against the pedestal sink and nearly fell into the claw-foot tub. But she managed to strip down, find some towels and rub her skin dry.

She chose a three-quarter-length, plaid flannel robe with buttons all the way up the front. The shoulders drooped halfway to her elbows, and she had to roll up the sleeves, but it was warm and comfortable. She hung her wet clothes over the shower curtain.

They reminded her that she needed to get back to Wichita Falls and check out of her hotel room. She couldn't keep wearing Katie's clothes, and she should really return the rental car.

She cringed, remembering the wires she'd yanked out of the motor. Should she confess the sabotage to Cole, or just wait until it was discovered and pay the damages? Hard to say. Ultimately, she'd rather give up money than mess up her chances with Cole.

She rubbed her hair dry and found a comb. Makeup, she'd have to do without.

When she wandered back into the living room, Cole's gaze slid down her body, lingering on her bare feet. He cleared his throat. "You want some socks?"

She glanced down at the billowing flannel. The tails hung past her knees. "You might have hit on the one way to make this outfit less attractive."

"You look fine."

"I look like a refugee from *Little House on the Prairie*."

Cole chuckled low. "Who cares? I'm a sure thing, remember?"

"That's an excellent point. I've never had a man see me at my worst and not had to care about it." She sat down in the big armchair and eased her saddle-sore legs under her. This was restful, in a bizarre sort of way.

All those years she'd spent fussing and primping and worrying. Cole could see her in a gunny sack and it wouldn't make a bit of difference. Come to think of it, this was pretty close to a gunny sack.

"This is your worst?" asked Cole.

She smoothed back her wet hair and nodded. "Pretty close."

"At least there'll be no surprises in our marriage." He headed into his bedroom.

Sydney leaned back into the soft cushions. He was forcing her to think past the wedding. What would they do? She had to take the Thunderbolt to New York. But what if Katie didn't get pregnant right away?

Would they keep up the charade? And if they did, would Sydney stay *here?*

She scanned the cabin again. It was a quaint little place. Maybe too quaint.

The kettle let out a shrill whistle. She waited a couple seconds, but Cole didn't appear. Finally she flipped off the blanket, groaned and straightened, then hustled toward the kitchen, nearly colliding with him as he appeared out of the bedroom.

He was shirtless. His feet were bare. And the button at the top of his clean jeans was undone, revealing a flash of skin below his washboard abs.

"Sorry." She put up her hand to forestall the collision and it came flat against his chest.

His fingers closed over her elbow to steady her and his thighs brushed up against hers.

"You okay?" he asked

She nodded, her heart skipping double-time. This was one good-looking cowboy. He looked great in his clothes, but out of them… Hoo, boy.

He reached over and shut off the burner.

Then his hand came up to cover hers, pressing it into his chest. His skin was warm and smooth. She could feel his heart thudding against his rib cage.

Her fingers made out the ridge of a horizontal scar. It was an uneven gash, three inches long, and she wondered what had happened.

From the little she'd seen of his life, she knew it was rough and physical. But what had caused this? And what other secrets were there on the body she'd admired for two days?

Before she could voice a question, their gazes met. His eyes turned a deep, ocean blue, and she inhaled his scent, marveling at how familiar it had become.

He slowly reached out to stroke her hair. Sensations washed over her like warm rain, and she longed to lean into him and absorb the full warmth of his strength. She held his gaze instead, finding flecks of gray among the storm-tossed blue. His look was turbulent, challenging.

He dipped his head ever so slightly. Then he stopped and his eyelids came down in a long blink.

"Is it just me?" he asked, refocusing. "Or is this a really stupid idea?"

She couldn't stop the slow, sultry smile that grew on her face. "It is a really stupid idea…"

His lips parted. "But…"

"Have we ever let that stop us before?"

Four

Cole was going to kiss this woman.

Stupid decisions were his stock-in-trade around her, and he saw no reason to give that up now.

"You're gorgeous," he said in all honesty, brushing the pad of his thumb across her cheek.

"So are you," she responded.

He grinned at that, sliding spread fingers through the thickness of her hair.

To his surprise, she rocked forward and placed a hot, moist kiss on his chest.

He sucked in a tight breath, and she kissed him again, her soft lips searing into his skin. It took a second to realize she was tracing the scar on his breastbone. She was kissing away his pain, soothing what was once a gaping wound, calming a memory he'd sworn he'd have to fight forever.

His hands convulsed and he tilted her head, searching her eyes for the reason behind her caring touch. What he saw was smoky jade and simmering passion.

Lightning exploded in the sky above them. Rain crashed down on the shake roof and clattered against the windowpanes. The oak trees creaked and the willows rustled as the wind whipped the world into a frenzy.

That same storm swirled to life inside him. He couldn't wait another second to taste her lips. He dipped to capture them, touching, tasting, savoring. They were as lush as he'd imagined, but sweeter, more giving, the perfect shape and size and pressure.

He kissed her again, this time pulling her soft body against his, opening wide, praying she'd follow suit. His skin was on fire and his chest tightened with a deep longing.

She parted her lips and a small moan escaped. The sound tugged at him, surrounded him, buried itself deep inside him as she wrapped her arms around his neck and hung on tight.

He inhaled her scent, wishing the moment could go on and on. He wanted to close his eyes, block out the world, lose himself in her, pretend nothing existed outside their cocoon.

But that was impossible.

The world did exist. The world of Kyle and Katie and the Thunderbolt. He slowly pulled back.

Her face was flushed and her eyes were glazed.

He suspected he looked exactly the same way.

She rubbed his chest and eased off with a deep breath. "Guess it's good to get that out of the way," she said.

"Our first kiss?"

She nodded, her gaze fixed somewhere below his neck. "Yeah. Could have been awkward in front of Katie."

"I'll say." He stepped back, raking a hand through his damp hair. "Now at least I'll know what to expect."

"Me, too."

"So it wasn't such a stupid idea after all."

"I think it was quite brilliant."

"Yes." He nodded. "Brilliant." He took a tight breath. "I'm, uh…" He gestured vaguely toward his bedroom door then escaped quickly and grabbed a clean shirt, stuffing his arms into the sleeves.

Brilliant was just the word. *Brilliant.* Now he wouldn't be able to look at her without getting aroused.

When he returned to the living room she was curled up in the armchair again with a pen and paper in her hands.

"We should talk logistics," she said.

Cole's steps faltered.

Maybe her mood could shift one-eighty in the blink of an eye, but he needed a few minutes to recover. He made a show of securing his buttons and tucking the shirt into his waistband, before he dropped down onto the couch and met her eyes.

"What have you got so far?" he asked, struggling to get back on an even keel, trying to ignore that fact that she was wearing his clothing.

She tucked her auburn hair behind one ear. It was beautiful even when it was wet.

"How fast do you think we can pull this off?" she asked.

"Why? You in a hurry?"

She glanced up in surprise. "Yes. I've got a whole display to coordinate. Dozens of pieces."

"I don't think Katie's going to buy love at first sight."

"I didn't mean this afternoon. It'll take a couple weeks to prepare the gallery."

"A whole two weeks?"

"Probably a little more."

Cole tamped down his annoyance at her business-like approach. They'd shared one kiss. Nothing had changed. There was still nothing more to their relationship than a commercial transaction.

"What's wrong?" she asked.

"Nothing." He neutralized his expression.

"You sure?"

"What could be wrong?"

She nodded. "Okay. Where's the Thunderbolt now?"

"In a lawyer's safe in Wichita Falls."

"Can we get it?"

"Not until after the wedding."

Sydney nodded again. "I'm going to need to make a few calls."

"Kyle has a land line at the house. So does Grandma." You couldn't pick up a cell signal in the Valley.

"You don't have a phone?"

Cole shrugged. "I only moved in after Kyle and Katie got married. Haven't updated much."

"No problem." Sydney flipped the page. "Okay. So what's our next move with Katie?"

"You might not want to takes notes on that."

"Why?"

He raised a brow.

"Oh. Right. We don't want to leave an evidence trail."

"Rain's stopping," Cole noted. "How about I drive you back to her place and you can wax poetic about me for a while?"

A slow smile grew on Sydney's face and Cole relaxed for the first time since the kiss.

"Let me see..." She began counting off on her fingers. "You are a good-looking guy. Smart, funny and oh—"

She snapped her fingers and laughed. "I can tell her you're sexy."

Cole wasn't sure how to take that. Was Sydney saying she thought he was sexy, or that she was willing to lie about it? He couldn't ask. It would sound stupid. And there was no logical reason for him to care.

Still, he couldn't help but wonder if she meant it.

When Katie found out Sydney was still checked into the hotel in Wichita Falls, she offered to drive her in to pick up her suitcase. The rental car was down for the count, and it was looking as though they'd need a tow truck to retrieve it. Exorbitantly expensive, but the drive alone with Katie seemed like a perfect opportunity to go all moony-eyed over Cole.

Not that it was such a huge stretch. That man could kiss like there was no tomorrow. She still got a little flushed thinking about it. In fact, she was hoping for an excuse to do it again. Soon.

The next morning, Katie's pickup truck bumped over the ruts of the ranch's access road.

"That's Grandma's house at the top of the hill," she said. "Kyle and Cole's dad grew up there. Kyle and Cole, too, for a while. But after the boys were born, their dad built the house where we live now."

"Cole mentioned his parents had died."

Katie nodded, gearing down to negotiate a series of potholes. "Light plane crash."

"Oh, no." A pain flashed through Sydney's chest, her mind going back to the horrible day when she'd learned her own parents had been killed in a house fire.

"Cole was in the plane," Katie continued. "He was the only one who lived."

"Was he all right?"

"Cuts, bruises, broken ribs. He was really lucky."

"But he lost his parents." And he had at least one scar to remind him. She was glad now she hadn't asked him about it.

Katie nodded again, keeping her gaze fixed on the road. "He's a good man, Sydney."

"I know he is."

"He's been through a lot."

"Yes, he has." Sydney understood better than most the horrible pain of losing your parents.

Katie cleared her throat. "I can understand…"

Sydney turned to try to gauge the odd tone of Katie's voice.

"I can understand that you might be tempted to, uh, romance the brooch from under—"

"Katie!"

"I'm not judging you. I have a sense of how important it is."

"I would *never*—"

"Like I said, I'm not judging. Women make choices all the time." Katie glanced at Sydney, a mixture of pain and awkwardness in her eyes. "I just don't want to see him hurt again."

Sydney frantically shook her head. "I've been completely honest and up-front with Cole."

"I saw how he looked at you."

"And I like him, too, Katie." Sydney's stomach clenched with guilt.

"He's falling for you."

"Maybe. I don't know." Sydney had to remind herself that she was being honest with Cole. She wasn't conning him, and she wouldn't hurt him.

"I don't know where this is going," she told Katie honestly. "But I won't lie to him about my feelings. I promise you."

"He's a good man," Katie said in a quiet voice.

"He's a very good man," Sydney agreed. "And he's lucky to have you."

Katie cracked a small smile.

Sydney reached out and touched her shoulder. "I'm serious, Katie. You are a terrific sister-in-law. Cole knows full well that I want the Thunderbolt. If anything happens between us, we'll both go into it with our eyes wide open."

Katie wiped her cheek with the back of her hand, giving Sydney a watery smile. "So, you think there might be a chance for the two of you?"

Sydney took a deep breath, turning back to the windshield as she chose her words. "I think Cole and I are going to have a very interesting relationship."

Sydney's answers must have satisfied Katie, because at the end of the day, Katie suggested stopping at her grandmother's for dinner. She said Saturday night was traditionally for family, and a perfect opportunity for Sydney to meet Grandma.

Cole had warned Sydney that his grandma was an incorrigible matchmaker, and that she'd go for broke the minute she laid eyes on Sydney. So Sydney was prepared for anything.

What she got was a sharp, funny, sweet-natured, little woman in a floppy hat and bright gardening gloves with a dream of a period house. Circa 1940, it had an octagonal entry hall, with an archway that led to a living room, while another doorway led to what looked like the master bedroom.

The wallpaper was yellowed and russet tiles were faded with age. But the wood trim shone with a dark patina and the leaded windows were definitely original.

"Your home is beautiful," Sydney said to Grandma, peering into the living room. The couch and armchair were burgundy, looped brocade, dotted with doilies that Sydney would bet Cole's grandmother had crocheted herself.

Grandma glanced around. "Never thought of it as beautiful before."

"It's *gorgeous,*" said Sydney, smiling at the incongruous wide-screen television and the personal computer perched on an antique, rolltop desk. Oh, how she'd love to check her e-mail.

"Sydney's here to visit for a few days," said Katie. "She's interested in the Thunderbolt of the North."

Sydney stole a quick glance at Katie, trying to decide if she was giving Grandma a subtle warning about her possible motives.

"Have to marry Cole to get the Thunderbolt," said Grandma as she led the way through the living room.

"So I understand," said Sydney.

They passed into a second octagonal hallway in the middle of the house, and then through a doorway to the kitchen at the back.

"Good news is that he's available," said Grandma.

"You know, he told me that himself."

Grandma looked back and cocked her head. "Did he, now?"

Sydney nodded.

The older woman smiled. She took a blue enamel kettle out of a painted cupboard and filled it with water from the deep, old-fashioned sink. "From New York, you say?"

"Yes."

"Like it here in Texas?"

"So far I'm having a wonderful time."

"That's good." Grandma nodded her head. "Cole's mother passed away, you know."

"Katie told me about that."

"His dad, too. My Neil."

"I'm very sorry."

"Well, I'm still here. And I've always figured that meant I've still got a job to do with one wayward grandson."

Sydney grinned, assuming she was in for the full court press. "You mean Cole or Kyle?"

"Cole, of course." Grandma paused. "You want to help me?" Then a split second later she gestured to a bowl of freshly picked blueberries so that the question could be interpreted either way.

"I'd love to help." Sydney was ready to give her all on both fronts.

"Good!" Grandma winked. "You can wash the berries. Katie, you get down a mixing bowl."

Katie opened a high cupboard and retrieved a large stoneware bowl. "Grandma's scones are renowned in this part of Texas."

"Recipe is a family secret," said Grandma. "Handed down from generation to generation."

"Can't wait to try them," said Sydney, pushing up the sleeves of her shirt.

"Grandma?" Katie ventured. "Why don't you explain to Sydney why the Thunderbolt goes to the wives?"

"I'll do that," said Grandma with a nod.

Katie turned to waggle an eyebrow at Sydney. "I love this story."

"Near as I can figure," said Grandma, scooping into a tin flour canister, "it started around the middle of the fourteenth century."

Sydney was instantly riveted. There was nothing she

liked better than family lore. As far as she was concerned, stories were as important as antiquities.

"The family went through a streak of good-for-nothing eldest sons," Grandma continued. "Worry was, if the young scoundrels got control of the Thunderbolt, they'd sell it for wenches and ale."

Sydney ran some water over the blueberries.

"Old Hendrik wanted to make sure they earned their money the Viking way," said Grandma, her practiced hands cutting a block of butter into the flour mixture. "By raiding and pillaging."

Sydney longed for a pen. She'd have to ask permission, of course, but she'd love to write this down for the museum.

"So, that's why Cole can't get the Thunderbolt until his wedding?" Sydney worked the stubby green stems off the berries.

"Can't have Cole going after ale and wenches," said Grandma with a wink and a sparkling smile.

"Do you have a lot of stories?" asked Sydney.

"Some," said Grandma.

"I'd love to hear them."

"And I love to talk. We'll get along just fine."

Grandma opened a drawer beneath the counter and pulled out a wooden rolling pin. "Berries ready?"

Sydney quickly turned her attention to the bowl, picking out the last of the stems, draining the water. Then she rolled the blueberries onto a clean towel.

"So, what do you say?" asked Grandma. "You willing to give my grandson a go?"

The front door slammed. "Grandma?" called Cole.

Grandma winked at Sydney again as she rolled out a round of dough. "That man needs a strong, intelligent woman," she stage-whispered.

Cole sauntered into the kitchen. "There you are." He gave his grandma a hug. He nodded to Katie. Then he clasped Sydney around the shoulders and gave her an affectionate squeeze. Good compromise.

"How was the trip?" he asked.

"Bought a Stetson and some blue jeans," said Sydney, finding it ridiculously easy to act excited about Cole's presence.

"Can't wait to see them." He dropped his arm from her shoulders and turned back to his grandma. "Need anything from the garden?"

"Potatoes and carrots," she answered.

"Want to help?" he asked Sydney.

"Sure."

Cole strode for the kitchen door, opening it and motioning for her to go first.

As she crossed the back deck to the stairs, she took in the spectacular panorama. She could see the roof of Cole's cabin, the winding creek, the blue-green lake and Katie and Kyle's house on a distant hill. Evergreens on the mountain ridges spiked up to a crackling turquoise sky.

"Be careful. They're steep," Cole warned from behind.

Sydney put her hand on the painted rail as she started down the long staircase that led to a lawn and a huge vegetable garden.

"How did it go?" Cole kept his voice low.

"Your grandma's definitely on board," said Sydney. "But Katie thought I was trying to romance the brooch out from under you."

Cole moved up beside her as they hit the bottom. "How do you know that?"

"She didn't pull any punches. She flat-out accused me of pretending to fall for you in order to get the Thunderbolt."

Cole shook his head, placing a hand on the small of Sydney's back and guiding her to the far side of the garden. "That Katie's more than just a pretty face."

"I'll say." His warm hand felt good against her back. It felt sure and strong. This chivalrous streak might be annoying in another man, but somehow it suited Cole. It wasn't put on and it wasn't a put-down. He was genuine. Genuine was nice.

"What did you tell her?"

"I swore up and down that I was being completely honest with you."

Cole grinned. "Good one. You're more than just a pretty face, too."

She stopped at the edge of the garden, telling herself he was just being polite. "Thank you. I may have a brain, but I'm not a gardener. What do we do?"

"I'm thinking something silly and romantic."

"What?"

"I can guarantee you they're watching us from the window." He picked a plump tomato from a vine and tossed it meaningfully in the air, catching it with one hand and advancing toward her with an evil grin.

She took a step back. "That doesn't look very romantic, Cole."

"I'm teasing you. Guys in love do that all the time."

"You stay back."

He kept advancing. "It's plump and ripe and very juicy."

She took another step backward and stumbled on a clump of grass. "Cole."

He lunged, and she shrieked, covering her eyes, expecting a face full of tomato juice. But he snaked an arm around her waist, pulling her up tight against his back, holding the tomato a safe distance away.

Guys in love. Cole did guys in love very, very well.

He kissed her neck. The heat of his lips and the puff of his breath made her knees go weak. She grabbed at his arm to support herself.

"Nice move," he whispered, kissing her again.

Oh, no. Her hormones surged to life. Her head dipped back to give him better access. The mountains blurred and the sound of cicadas magnified in the long grass.

"Sydney," he breathed, and she turned to meet his lips.

The world instantly shrank to the two of them. She'd been thinking about this all day, missing this all day, every second she was in Wichita Falls, every second she'd been away from Cole.

She couldn't understand it, but nor could she deny it that his kisses seemed the center of the universe. The world pulsated out from the moisture of his lips, the touch of his hands. He lowered them slowly to the soft, fragrant grass, released the tomato and wrapped his arms fully around her.

She closed her eyes. The afternoon sun heated her skin, soaked into her hair. Cole was a delicious weight on top of her, and his lips were working magic. She needed to stay here, just another second, just another minute.

Somebody cleared their throat.

Sydney's eyes flew open and a pair of worn boots came into focus. She squinted up to where Kyle's Stetson blocked the sun.

"Much as I admire your dedication to the cause," he drawled, "I think you two might be overacting."

Cole eased his weight off her.

"Sorry," said Sydney, adjusting her shirt. Where exactly had Cole's hands roamed? What had Kyle seen?

Cole rolled to his feet and held out a hand for Sydney. "Just trying to do our part," he said to Kyle.

Kyle fought a grin. "Next time get a room."

"What would be the point in that?" asked Cole.

Kyle glanced at Sydney and snorted before turning away.

Cole pulled her into a standing position and patted her on the back. "Way to go, partner."

She smoothed her hair. "No problem." No problem at all. If that was Cole faking it, some lucky woman was going to live in paradise someday.

Cole scooped his hat from the ground. "Potatoes and carrots."

"You think that was overkill?" she asked.

"Nah. It was romantic."

"So you figure we're getting it right."

He walked into the garden and crouched down. "Aside from you making Katie suspicious, I think it's going according to plan."

Sydney turned to watch Kyle stride up the staircase. "You know, you three blow me away."

"What do you mean?" Cole dug into the black dirt.

"Katie's protecting you from me. Kyle's protecting his wife from stress. And you're compromising your principles to help them both."

"Something wrong in that?"

"Something nice in that. I'm just trying to save my job." She liked what that said about Cole. She wasn't completely sure she liked what that said about her.

Cole rose to his feet, dusting one hand off on the thigh of his jeans as he made his way out of the garden. "Your job is in jeopardy?"

She nodded. "Yeah," she admitted. "I'm on probation. There's this guy…"

Then she stopped herself and shook her head. She wasn't letting thoughts of Bradley mar the day. "Truth is,

I haven't been delivering the way the museum needs. If the Thunderbolt hadn't worked out, I'd have been out of a job."

"Hold these." He filled her hands with long, crisp carrots. "So, do I get extra points for helping you *and* with Katie?"

"Absolutely." She tried to think of something nice she could do for Cole. "You want to come to New York and see the display?"

He shrugged, heading into another section of the garden. "Maybe. If we're still faking it."

Sydney watched Cole unearth a handful of potatoes and tried to imagine him in her Sixth Avenue apartment. He was too big for New York, too raw, too wild. He belonged on horseback in the rain, or half naked in his cabin kitchen.

She shivered at that particular memory. This urge to kiss him was turning into an obsession. And the obsession was moving way past kissing.

Cole was untamable and exciting and exotic. He was sexy as all get-out, and challenged her on every level. Aside from the Thunderbolt, aside from the charade, she wanted him in every way a woman could possibly want a man.

"You'll never get anyone to marry you without a decent house," said Grandma, plunking a well-thumbed catalog down on the low table in front of him.

Cole snapped to attention, pulling his arm from the back of the porch swing where he'd been toying with Sydney's hair. "Huh?"

"I've been after you for months to pick out plans. And with Sydney here, well, it seems like the perfect opportunity to get a female opinion."

"As opposed to yours and Katie's?" Cole wasn't picking out house plans. He had other things to spend his money on, and he had a perfectly good cabin down by the creek.

"Great idea," said Katie, pulling her patio chair closer. Her eyes shone with anticipation as she flipped open the book.

"Cape Cod or Colonial?" asked Kyle, placing his hands on his wife's shoulders.

Cole glared at his brother. "I do not need a new house."

"You're joking, right?" said Katie.

She shifted her attention to Sydney. "Tell him no self-respecting woman would live in that cabin."

Sydney tensed, and Cole automatically reached out to squeeze her hand. "You're putting Sydney on the spot, Katie."

Grandma sidled up next to Sydney. "I'm sure she doesn't mind. We just want to take advantage of your cosmopolitan taste, dear."

Sydney kept her mouth shut tight, and Cole shot Kyle a meaningful glare. Unfortunately his brother's only response was a mocking grin.

"I need a new hay barn," said Cole. "An addition on the tack shed, and an upgrade to the combines. We all agreed in the spring."

"No. *You* agreed in the spring," said Katie primly. "The rest of us thought you needed a new house."

Cole reached out and shut the book. He'd agreed to a marriage of convenience. He'd agreed to pretend it was real. But he wasn't building any damn house just to keep Katie from being stressed.

"The cabin's fine," he said, moderating his voice. "Even if I was to get married—" he turned to Sydney "—that cabin would be okay in the short term. Right?"

She swallowed. "Uh—"

Katie jerked the catalog out from under Cole's hand.

"Now you're the one putting Sydney on the spot. If the cabin's so fine, we'll move into it. You take the house."

"Don't be ridiculous."

"Why is it ridiculous when I say it?"

"There are two of you. And you're a woman."

"Now you're sounding sexist."

Cole turned to his brother. "You'd actually let your wife live in the cabin."

"Nope," said Kyle. "But it sounds like you're willing to let yours."

Cole opened his mouth, but he couldn't immediately come up with the right argument. Damn Kyle. This was *not* his opportunity to push the new house agenda.

"And what about the children?" asked Katie. "There's absolutely no room in the cabin for children."

All eyes swung to Sydney. "Maybe an addition?" she offered.

Katie laughed. "Yeah, right. Cape Cod or Colonial?"

Grandma patted her hand. "Don't be shy, Sydney. We value your input."

Sydney hesitated, but she was being stared down by the entire family. "I've, uh, always liked a nice Cape Cod."

"Page thirty-nine," said Grandma.

"Well, you were a big help," Cole said to Sydney as they walked down the ranch road in the moonlight. After her initial protest, she'd plunged into the planning session with gusto.

"I tried to keep quiet."

"And that didn't seem to work out for you?"

"I'm supposed to be falling for you, so I tried to make myself sound like actual wife material. I answered all your Grandma's questions. We swapped recipes—"

"You know recipes?"

Sydney shot him a look. "I made them up. Point is, if I'd balked at planning my future house, it would have looked suspicious."

"Now they're going to want me to build the damn thing."

"So what? The cabin is falling apart."

"What am I going to do with a two-story, octagonal great room?"

"I didn't vote for the octagonal great room. That was Katie."

"Well you voted for the dormer windows."

"They're pretty."

"And a turret?"

"Adds detail."

"And what am I going to do with a hot tub?"

Sydney was silent for a moment. "Uh, bathe?"

"Very funny. I don't need jets and bubblers rumbling under my butt to get clean."

"Ever tried one?"

"No."

She grinned and bumped her shoulder against his arm. "Don't know what you're missing, cowboy."

"Why? Have you?"

"It just so happens I *own* a hot tub."

A visual bloomed in Cole's brain—of Sydney, glistening skin and swirling water.

"Cole?"

He cleared his throat. "Yeah?"

"You ever stop to think there might be some deep-seated, psychological reason you shortchange yourself?"

"No." He didn't shortchange himself, and he didn't have deep-seated reasons for anything. He herded cows. He raised horses. He kept the ranch running. What you saw was what you got.

"You're living in a cabin where you wouldn't let any other member of your family live."

That wasn't true. He turned from the ranch road down his short driveway and the roar of the creek grew louder. "I'd let Kyle live there."

"And you've never been married."

"Lucky for you." If he was married she wouldn't be getting this opportunity with the Thunderbolt.

"See, I have a hard time believing women aren't interested in you. If you'd wanted—"

"Plenty of women are interested in me." He felt ego-bound to point that out. Well, maybe not plenty. But some. Enough. He wasn't exactly a monk out here.

"Then why haven't you settled down?"

"It's not by choice."

"Bet it is."

"Not my choice."

"The women said no?"

He refused to answer, wondering how he and Sydney always ended up having such personal conversations. He was a private man. He liked it that way.

"Come on, Cole," Sydney prompted.

"Why aren't *you* married?" He tried to turn the tables.

Her answer surprised him. "Nobody ever proposed."

"Did you even want them to?" he asked.

"You mean, have I ever been in love?"

"Yeah."

"I don't think so."

"You don't know?" That surprised Cole.

She shook her head. "What about you?"

"I guess not."

She grinned and bumped him again. "But *you're* not sure?"

He cocked his head, considering her. "You know, it's hard, isn't it? To know for sure."

"Is that why you never asked anyone."

"Nah. Never got that far. Truth is, they all left me once they got to know me."

She tipped her head back and gave him a hint of that sexy laugh. "No way. You left them."

He had to squelch an urge to wrap his arm around her. She was just the right height, just the right size, just the right shape for his arms.

Instead he shook his head. "I'm a bit of a selfish jerk deep down inside."

"No. You're the opposite. Just like I said. You're the one sacrificing to take care of everyone around you."

They came to the porch and he preceded her up the three steps. "Do you happen to have a degree in psychology?"

"I have a degree in art history."

"Good." He pushed open the door and stood to one side. "You can decorate the turret and leave my brain alone."

She grinned as she walked past him. "Your brain is beginning to fascinate me."

"I don't want a new house, because I don't need a new house. This is a working ranch, not a Dallas subdivision. Next thing they'll be putting in a pool."

"I've hit on something here, haven't I?"

"You haven't hit on anything." His voice came out unexpectedly sharp as he flipped the kitchen lamp.

Her eyes went wide. "I'm sorry."

Cole swore under his breath. He shook his head and moved toward her. "No. I'm the one who's sorry." He was falling back on defense mechanisms now.

"It's none of my business," she said.

"Of course it's not. But we're playing this silly game." He took a breath. "Ah, Sydney. We should have known it would get complicated."

She gave him a nod and a hesitant smile, and he found himself easing closer. He inhaled deeply, filling his senses.

Her lips were burgundy in the lamplight. Her emerald eyes were fringed by thick lashes. Her skin was ivory-smooth, flushed from the walk. And the memory of it was indelibly pressed into the nerves of his fingertips.

Unable to stop himself, he smoothed a lock of hair from her forehead.

"Complicated," he whispered one more time.

Her lips parted, softly, invitingly. He should have known the second he got her alone, he'd give in to the cravings. He cupped her cheeks, pulling her closer. His lips closed over hers and relief roared through his body.

He'd been watching her all day, wanting her all day. She was under his skin and into his brain in a way that he couldn't control.

He kissed her harder, stepping toward her, pressing her back against the door. A bronc had blasted off inside him, and there was nothing he could do but hang on for the ride.

He tipped his head to find a better angle, and she came alive under his hands, all movement and sound and scent.

This was good. This was right. This was more than he'd ever found in any other woman. He stopped thinking about the Thunderbolt. He stopped thinking about Katie. He stopped thinking about plots and plans and deceptions.

There was only Sydney, her taste and her touch.

"Cole," she breathed, her fingertips tightening on his shoulders.

"I know." He kissed her eyelids.

"This *is* complicated."

"This is inevitable."

She paused for a second. "Maybe."

"Absolutely." He slipped his hand under her shirt, skimming across the small of her back. Her skin was sinfully warm, sinfully soft. She was a treasure he hadn't earned and didn't deserve.

"We can stop," he whispered reassuringly, kissing his way along the crook of her neck. "You say when."

"Not yet," she whispered back.

"Thank God," he sighed.

Her hand inched its way slowly up between them and, one by one, she popped the buttons on his shirt. When the last one gave way, she burrowed inside the fabric.

He kissed the top of her head and rocked her in his arms. He wanted to carry her to his bed, press himself against her—kiss her, talk to her, make love with her, simply breathe the same air. Whatever she wanted, whenever she wanted it.

She kissed his chest, her hot tongue flicking out to sear his skin.

He struggled for air as passion commandeered his senses. "We're pushing it," he warned.

She kissed him again. "Let's push it further."

He pulled back and gazed down at her. Her lips were swollen, her eyes were slumberous and her hair was tousled out like a halo.

"You want to make love?" he asked.

"Yeah."

"You sure?"

She smoothed her palms up the front of his chest. "You're right. It's inevitable."

Five

Sydney held her breath, wondering if Cole might actually refuse.

"I want you *so* bad," he said instead.

Her breath whooshed out. "You had me worried there for a second, cowboy."

He shook his head, smoothing back her hair. "Don't you worry. Don't you ever worry."

Something settled deep inside her and her worries vanished.

Cole had to be the most honest and honorable man she'd ever met. Yeah, he was getting in her way over the Thunderbolt. But he was doing it out of respect for his family.

Unlike the men she'd dated in New York, unlike some of her colleagues and contacts at the museum, everything she'd seen, everything he'd done, told her Cole was a man to be trusted.

She'd missed trust.

She'd missed honor.

She wanted him and he wanted her. It didn't get much more honest than that.

She focused on the feel of his rough palm against her scalp. His eyes burned smoky-blue, and she felt like the most desirable woman in the world. Her lashes grew heavy and she tilted her head into the sensation of Cole.

His palm cupped her face and he kissed her eyes. Her body felt as if it were drifting on air, soaring up to the ceiling. The dying fire gave off a faint, distinct tang. The creek roared over boulders outside the window, and Cole left trails of shooting sparks wherever he touched.

She tasted his salty skin, then she squeezed his hard body tighter and tighter until she was safe and surrounded by his warmth. He lifted her into his arms as if she weighed nothing. Nobody had ever carried her before. He started to walk, and she was sorry the bedroom was so close.

"Hold me for a minute," she said when they got there.

His arms flexed. "No problem."

She sighed against his chest. "You think you could stop time? Right here? Right now?"

"I wish I could."

"Try really, really hard."

His chuckle rumbled through her. "I can go slow."

"Easy for you, maybe."

"Nope. Not easy at all."

"But you'd do it for me?"

"I'll do anything for you. Just say the word."

Let me into your world, she wanted to say. Not just your bed, but your heart and your soul.

But that was impossible. They had here and now, and that was all. She forced a light note into her voice.

"Get naked."

"Okay. But that might speed things up a little."

"Or I could get naked."

"That would be worse." His voice sounded strangled.

She struggled to push his shirt from his shoulders. "Let's play with fire."

He slowly lowered her feet to the floor. "Sydney, I've been playing with fire since the first second I laid eyes on you."

She took a shaky step back and reached for the hem of her T-shirt. He stared down at her with such longing and reverence that a shudder ran straight through her body. She peeled the shirt over her head, gauging his reaction, loving his reaction.

His nostrils flared and his gaze latched onto her lacy bra. Without a word, he shucked his own shirt.

She stared unabashedly at the play of muscles across his chest. "You think we want this so bad, because we know we shouldn't?"

"Yeah." He nodded. "It probably has nothing to do with the way you look, taste, smell or feel."

"That's it."

"That's what?"

"The way you smell."

"It's bad?"

She shook her head, gliding toward him, burying her face in his chest again. "It's good. So good."

He reached between their bodies and flicked the button on her jeans. "You, too."

She smiled and went on her toes, kissing his mouth as he lowered her zipper. "Let's not tell anyone," she said.

"That we made love?"

She shook her head. "The smell secret."

"You got it."

He rolled off her pants then got rid of his own. Then he gently pressed her back on the bed, covering her with kisses, whispering words of reverence and encouragement, sending her heart rate soaring and her hormones into overdrive.

His fingertips skimmed her stomach, circling her navel with a featherlight touch that made her breath come in a gasp and her muscles contract. Before she could adjust to the sensation, he bent over her breast, taking one nipple into his mouth, swirling and circling the crest with his tongue.

She moaned, and her hands went to his hair. Sensations rocketed through her body as his teeth raked her tender flesh and his hand began a downward spiral.

This wasn't going to be slow. It was going to be lightning fast if she didn't do something.

"Cole," she gasped.

"You're delicious," he answered, fingers dipping lower, increasing the onslaught of sensation.

"Slow…down…" she begged.

She felt his smile. "No way." He crossed the downy curls and pressed into her in one swift motion.

Her hips came up off the bed, and her hands convulsed against his head. "Cole," she wailed.

"Go with it," he said.

"But…"

He moved to look into her eyes, his fingers pulsing in a way that made her world shift to the exquisite touch on her tender, moist flesh. She flexed her hips. He kissed her mouth.

"There's more to come," he rumbled against her. "I promise."

She closed her eyes. She was past the point of resisting. Past the point of coherent thought. She was going where he led her, and there was no way to stop it.

Her world roared, then went silent.

They were skin to skin, soul to soul as he eased inside her. True to his word, he took it slow, watching her closely, gauging her desires. Their breathing synchronized as the corner clock ticked away minutes.

A warm rush of sensation crested up from her toes. He smiled and deepened his kiss, increasing his rhythm until her world imploded, the clock's ticks slowed to a crawl and paradise stretched on and on.

She wrapped her arms around his neck, guilt nipping at her conscience. Nobody had ever done that before. No one had ever set aside their own needs to take her to paradise.

As the power of speech returned, she searched his deep eyes, worried that he'd made some stupid, gentlemanly decision against making love. "We're not...uh...stopping, are we?"

He shook his head and brushed a lock of hair from her cheek, shifting so that his big body covered hers. "Oh, sweetheart. We're just getting started."

He kissed her mouth. His thumb returned to her breast and, against all odds, her desire instantly rallied.

She ran her hands down his back, sliding them onto his taut buttocks and pressing his erection against her stomach, shivering with anticipation. She kissed his harder, swirling her tongue against his.

He opened wide, and she could feel the tension rising in his muscles.

She moaned and wriggled beneath him, shifting her thighs in a clear invitation.

He gasped. "Hey. This is supposed to be the slow part."

"Fast is fun," she assured him, shifting again, even more meaningfully this time.

He grabbed her hip with a broad hand and held her still,

pulling back to look into her eyes. "If I go now, I'm going to break a land-speed record."

"Now," she said. "I don't care. Now." Slow had been a stupid idea anyway. Nothing between her and Cole was ever going to be slow.

He flexed his hips and was instantly inside her.

She groaned, nearly melting around his heat.

He buried his hands in her hair, thumbs stroking her temples. His breath came in gasps next to her ear.

She could feel the tension cresting in his steel, hard muscles. Her body tightened and strained and pulsated.

She reached for the comfortor, fisting her hands into the fabric as their rhythm increased.

He repeated her name, over and over again. Then his hands found hers, covered hers, their fingers entwining as the world exploded into black and time ceased to exist.

Cole kissed her damp brow. "You okay?"

She sighed, sinking into his incredibly soft bed. "I don't think okay is exactly the right word."

"You hurt?"

"No. It's fantastic. Fantastic is the right word."

He chuckled low in her ear, easing most of his weight off her. "You give me heart failure all the time, you know that?"

"You're pushing things too fast," said Kyle as he tapped the remainder of the glass from a broken window in the toolshed.

Cole set a new pane on the ground, leaning it against the wall of the shed before he retrieved a hammer from the toolbox.

Kyle didn't know the half of how fast they'd pushed things. Cole had never done that before—made love after only two days.

"I think we're doing fine," he said, strapping on a leather belt and dumping a handful of nails into the pouch.

Kyle whacked at a stubborn corner of glass and it tinkled into jagged pieces. "First you're necking on the lawn, then you bring her home after midnight."

A grin split Cole's face. "Will you listen to yourself? You sound like her father."

"I'm just saying, Katie's not going to buy it if you don't slow it down."

Cole moved up to the shed wall and dug his claw hammer into the window frame. One by one, the finishing nails popped out. "It's a compromise. Sydney's on a deadline with the Thunderbolt."

"You're worried about her deadline? This from a guy who was willing to throw her off the property two days ago?"

"I'm getting to know her now. And I didn't realize her job was on the line."

Kyle stopped, fixing his attention on Cole. "She told you her job was on the line?"

"Yeah."

Kyle glared at him impatiently.

"What?"

"Cole. What are you doing?"

Had Kyle guessed what had happened last night? Was it that obvious?

"I'm pretending to fall for Sydney," he said with exaggerated patience, trying to gauge his brother's expression.

"You sure about that?"

"I'm positive about that. What are you suggesting?"

Kyle whacked the glass again. "I'm suggesting you watch yourself."

Cole nearly choked on that one. "Hang on. This was *your* idea, little brother."

"Yeah." Kyle tugged his leather work gloves from his back pocket. "And I may have been wrong about that."

"Wrong? Hello? What did I miss?"

"She could be playing you," said Kyle, settling his fingers in the grooves.

"Playing me how? She's been up front and honest about everything." Unlike him and Kyle who were pulling one over on Katie.

"Has she?"

"Yes!"

Kyle brushed shards of glass from the sill. "Think about it, Cole. She's getting exactly what she came for."

"Uh, yeah. That was the deal."

"The deal was Katie would think Sydney fell for you. But now *you* think Sydney's falling for you."

"No, I don't," Cole snapped.

"Yes, you do. And what the hell are the odds of that?"

Cole hadn't honestly thought about the odds last night. But then, he didn't think Sydney was falling for him, either. Not really. It was more a chemical thing. A very powerful chemical thing.

Not that he could tell Kyle he'd slept with Sydney. How suspicious would that look?

"It's under control," he said to Kyle.

"You telling me you're not falling for her?"

"We're faking it for Katie."

"You and I shared a room for fifteen years, Cole. Quite frankly, you're not that good an actor."

"So, what are you suggesting? I call it off? Kick her out?"

"I'm just suggesting you watch your back. Don't trust her too far too soon."

"Fine."

"I'm serious."

"I said fine."

"Just think about the possibilities."

Cole dug in on the upper frame. "What part of *fine* didn't you understand?"

He would think about the possibilities. He was thinking about the possibilities. Because he didn't know Sydney.

Yeah, he felt as though he knew her. But she had an agenda, and that agenda included getting him to the altar.

What he'd interpreted as sweet, sexy vulnerability, could have been cold, calculated manipulation. Maybe she was hot for him, or maybe she was playing to his ego.

As bad as it sucked, Kyle had a point. What *were* the odds of a woman like Sydney wanting to sleep with a man like Cole after only two days?

Katie had offered Sydney the use of Kyle's office phone to contact the museum. Sydney's heart thumped in her chest as she dialed Gwen Parks's number. Saying it out loud was going to make it real.

"Gwen, here," came her friend's voice over the phone line.

"Hey, Gwen. It's Sydney."

"Hey, Sydney." There was a smile in Gwen's voice. "How's the hunt going?"

Sydney took a deep breath. "Well. I found it."

There was silence on the other end of the line. "Define 'it.'"

"The Thunderbolt of the North."

Gwen squealed and Sydney jerked the phone away from her ear.

"You actually found it? Where are you? Where is it? What happened?"

"I'm in Texas."

Another silence.

"Who'd have thought," said Sydney.

"Did you bring it over from Europe?"

"It's been here the whole time."

"Oh, wow. When are you coming back?"

Sydney lowered her voice. "Not right away. It's complicated. Can I get you started on the show?"

"Without you?"

"Yeah."

"Of course. But you *do* have the Thunderbolt, right?"

"It's in a lawyer's office in Wichita Falls. But don't tell a soul. Bradley Slander is still gunning for me, and I don't want him getting wind of this until it's a done deal."

"If it's not a done deal, why am I setting up the show?"

Sydney twisted the phone cord around her hand. "It is. Sort of. Well… I have to marry the owner."

Another silence.

"It's a complicated inheritance thing."

"You're going to *marry* into the Thunderbolt family?"

"It's a marriage of convenience."

"Don't you think that's above and beyond?"

"It's the only way. I'm pretending to fall…" Sydney hesitated over the details. "Anyway, we'll divorce as soon as the show's over."

"I don't know, Sydney."

"Trust me on this. I've got it under control. My notes on the other antiquities are in my computer, along with the contact names. I'm going to reserve the front gallery."

"You're making me nervous."

"I can do this."

"You sure?"

"Yes."

She had to do this. She had no choice but to do this. It didn't matter how complicated her feelings got for Cole.

Nor did it matter how much she was starting to love this crazy Texas ranch.

She was here to do a job. Once she got back to New York it would all fall into perspective. She'd be hailed a hero, and her professional reputation would be saved.

"Okay."

"Great. Talk to you in a few days." Sydney let out a sigh of relief and hung up the phone.

It was going to happen. It was truly going to happen.

Then she glanced up, and there was Katie, white-faced in the doorway.

Damn. She opened her mouth, but Katie turned on her heel.

"Katie!" Sydney scrambled around the desk, sprinting to the door. "Katie, it's not what—"

"Don't!" Katie gritted her teeth, her hands balling into fists as she stomped down the hallway. "You lied to me. You lied, straight-faced, and I let you into my family."

"Cole knows."

"Yeah, right."

"He *knows*."

Katie shook her head, her voice quavering. "No, he doesn't. But he's going to. Right now."

She stormed out the door and Sydney took off after her.

The plan was ruined. Sydney had screwed up everything. She should have talked quieter. She should have closed the door.

Cole was going to kill her, and so was Kyle, and now Katie would be more stressed than ever.

"Katie, listen," she gasped, rushing through the open doorway and struggling to catch up. She tried running, but her pace in heels was no match for Katie in her boots. Katie easily outdistanced her to the toolshed.

"She's a con artist and a liar and thief," yelled Katie as Sydney rapidly approached the three.

Kyle dropped a tool onto the ground and wrapped his arms around his wife. "What the hell?"

"She overheard me," Sydney called as she made her way through cacti and range grass.

"She's pretending to fall in love with Cole." Katie's voice broke. "I heard her. She's only after the Thunderbolt."

Cole stuffed a hammer into his tool belt and moved toward Katie, laying a hand on her shoulder. "It's okay, Katie. I know that already."

"How could you know that?" she sniffed. "She's lying to you. She's lying to all of us." She shot Sydney a look of venom.

"I am so sorry," said Sydney, her voice shaking, a sick feeling swirling in the pit of her stomach.

"I'll just bet you are," Katie snapped.

"Sweetheart." Kyle spoke against her hair in a soft voice. "This is all my fault."

Katie tipped her chin to look up at him. "How is it your fault?"

Sydney wished the ground would open up and swallow her whole. Katie was such a wonderful human being. She didn't deserve this heartache. She deserved Kyle's love every minute of every day, plus a whole troop of little Ericksons running around her house.

"*I* did something really stupid," said Cole.

"It was *me,*" said Sydney. She didn't want to break up this happy family. They loved each other. They meant the world to each other.

"Will you two stop?" asked Kyle.

"Katie," said Cole. "After the baby thing—"

Katie turned a shade paler.

"—I thought your stress level would drop if I got married and had babies."

"We weren't really going to have babies," Sydney put in. "We were just going to let you think we'd have babies. It seemed like the perfect plan. I'd get the Thunderbolt. You'd probably get pregnant. By the time we got divorced, you'd be okay again."

Katie turned to Kyle. "You went along with this?"

"I—"

"We talked him into it," said Cole. "*I* talked him into it. Thing is, Katie. I'm going to make it come true."

The breath rushed from Sydney's lungs and she blinked at Cole's rugged profile. Because of last night? Because of what they'd shared?

Was it possible? Did Cole think there was something growing between them?

Her chest expanded with a warm glow. She had no idea how they'd work it out, but the thought of Cole wanting to try settled around her like a soft blanket.

"As soon as I divorce Sydney," Cole continued, and Sydney's heart went flat, "I'm going to find another wife. A real wife. I'm going to take on some of the responsibility of this damn dynasty."

Cole's words died away to silence and Sydney took an involuntary step back.

Of course he'd find a real wife. What on earth was she thinking? Cole couldn't do New York, and Sydney wasn't staying in Texas. Her career and her life were about to take a quantum leap. The sky would be the limit after the Thunderbolt show.

Katie stared at her, and Sydney forced out a shaky laugh. "See? It'll all work out."

"Cole," said Kyle. "You don't have—"

"My mind's made up." Cole rubbed Katie's shoulder. "I just hope I can find a wife who'll hold a candle to you."

Katie wiped her cheeks with the back of her hand. "I'm sorry," she whispered to Sydney.

Sydney moved closer. "You have absolutely nothing to be sorry about." Katie had come to a perfectly logical conclusion.

She nodded her agreement. "Okay. But we probably shouldn't tell Grandma it's a sham."

Cole looked at Kyle, and Kyle looked at Cole.

"You're right," said Cole. "We still have a wedding to plan."

Sydney parked herself on an old workbench to watch Cole finish the window repair. It had seemed like a good idea to give Katie and Kyle some time alone. She wanted to ask Cole about his marriage promise, but she didn't want him to think she cared.

If she didn't care, would she ask or stay quiet? Hard to know. Probably ask. After all, it was all academic to her.

She made up her mind. "Cole?"

"Yeah?"

"Were you serious? Or were you just trying to make Katie happy?"

"Serious about what?"

"Finding a real wife." She hated the pain that flashed through her chest when she said those words. It was almost as though she was jealous. Which made no sense. She was never going to see Cole again after the museum show. That had always been the plan.

Just because she'd slept with him, she didn't need to get all moony-eyed about it. She'd slept with men before. Men she'd liked and trusted. But she'd never gone around the bend over it. She'd never started imagining forever. Never even been jealous of the women they *might* date in the future.

Cole nodded as he hammered tiny nails around the wood that held the new glass. "I am putting too much pressure on Kyle and Katie. It's time I held up my end of the family."

"Do you think planning to marry some unknown wife is such a good idea?"

He stopped hammering and gave her a long look. "Yes, I do."

"It doesn't strike you as just a little bit self-sacrificing?"

He went back to hammering. "Not really. We Texans take loyalty and honor very seriously."

Sydney shifted on the bench. "Ouch."

Cole shrugged. "Not a criticism."

"Yeah, right." Obviously her values were a question mark in his mind. She might be fine for a night in bed, but she sure didn't meet his standards for a wife.

Good girl, bad girl again. At least this time she knew which one she was.

"We can probably move the marriage plans up," he said.

Sydney nodded. "That's good." The sooner she got away from him, the better.

"If Grandma suspects anything," he continued, "it'll be that you're pregnant and we need a quickie wedding."

"But you've only known me a few days."

He pounded in a final nail and dropped the hammer into his belt. "I travel a lot. She'll assume we've met before."

"Of course." Sydney nodded. Because a bad girl is always good for a one-night stand when a guy's on the road. She gritted her teeth and forced herself to focus on business. "I've asked a colleague to start preparing for the show."

Cole gave a nod.

"Is there any way I could take a look at the Thunderbolt before the wedding?"

"I guess so. What for?"

"It'll help me conceptualize a display for it. It would really help if I could take a couple of pictures to send to the museum." Business, business. All business. She could do this.

Cole stood back to scrutinize the job. "I'll drive you in as soon as I can get away."

Six

One thing about having Katie in on the marriage plan, it meant Sydney didn't have to see nearly as much of Cole. While she waited for the trip to Wichita Falls, she made museum arrangements by long distance and spent some time visiting Grandma.

Sydney was growing to like the eccentric old woman. Grandma was smart, opinionated and had one zinger of a sense of humor. She also told stories about the Thunderbolt and about her early years in Texas that fascinated Sydney.

Like the time the pack string stepped in a wasps' nest. The first horse through was stung once and did a little crow hop off the trail. His burden of flour and utensils stayed put. The second horse through was a bomb-proof mare. She barely flinched when three wasps stung her rump.

Unfortunately, the third horse through took the brunt of the attack. He was a reliable four-year-old entrusted with the month's supply of whiskey. The horse leapt off the ground, all four feet in the air. His frantic bucking loosened the pack saddle, sending the whiskey swinging under his belly.

The unnatural load spooked him even more, and he ran hell bent for leather into the creek. Though the cowboys raced to his rescue, the precious cargo was washed over the falls.

The cook was so frightened at the prospect of showing up at the cattle drive without a fresh whiskey supply that he rode two days and two nights to restock.

When Cole finally announced he had time to take Sydney to the city, she eagerly hopped into his pickup. She couldn't wait to see the Thunderbolt, even if it meant a two-hour drive alone with him.

"Haven't seen much of you," he commented as they pulled onto the main road.

"Haven't seen much of you, either," she returned, gauging his tone, wondering how to read him and annoyed that she felt the need to try.

He shrugged. "Had work to do."

"Me, too." She did have a life. It wasn't as if she'd been pining away, wondering if he regretted their lovemaking, or if he'd found any likely Susie Homemakers to take her place.

"Have I done something to annoy you?" he asked.

Did he mean other than announce to his family that he was finding a "real" wife just as soon as he dumped her?

"I'm not annoyed," she said.

"So this is the level you've picked for our relationship?"

The level *she'd* picked? "You wanted something more?"

He shrugged, flipping on his right signal and leaving the gravel road behind in favor of the four-lane interstate. "You must admit, it all turned on a dime there after Katie got in the loop."

"Ah." Sydney nodded, wishing she could control the jealousy cresting in her veins. "So you did want more sex."

He twisted his head to look at her. "Excuse me?"

"Sorry about that. I guess I did turn off the tap all of a sudden."

His eyes narrowed, and he glanced to the highway and back to her again. "Was there a particular reason you backed off?"

She shrugged. No reason that was remotely logical, just a horrible, kicked-in-the-gut feeling when he'd rejected her. "We didn't need to pretend anymore," she said.

"You mean, the Thunderbolt was in the bag."

"Yeah. Right. Something like that." She turned her head to look out the window.

"I see."

"Okay."

"Fine." He pressed on the accelerator and turned up the radio.

Neither of them spoke until they hit Wichita Falls.

At a traffic light in the heart of downtown, Cole turned on the left turn signal and waited for a space in traffic. "This is it."

Despite his brooding presence, Sydney's stomach leaped in anticipation. "Which one?"

He pointed to a tall, gray office tower as he angled into a parking spot in front.

Sydney scanned the building. This was it. The treasure of a lifetime was waiting inside for her. Despite her anger with Cole, she felt like a kid on Christmas morning.

They entered the building and took an elevator to the tenth floor. The brass sign on the oversize office doors read Neely And Smythe, Attorneys-At-Law.

"Auspicious," said Sydney.

"It's been the family firm for four generations."

"And the Thunderbolt's been here the whole time?"

"Most of it."

"I'm getting goose bumps."

As he opened the door, Cole gave her his first smile in three days.

It felt good. Way too good. Pathetically good.

She preceded him into the reception area, and a smiling brunette woman greeted them warmly. She sat behind a marble counter in a room decorated with leather furniture and fine art.

"Mr. Neely can see you right away," she said to Cole.

Cole moved to open another doorway that took them to a private hall.

A balding man met them at the far end of the hallway. He shook hands with Cole then turned to Sydney. "Joseph Neely." He offered his hand to her. "I understand you're here to see the Thunderbolt."

"I am," she agreed. "Sydney Wainsbrook."

"I enjoy an excuse to look at it myself," he said, turning his key in the lock and pushing the door inward.

"It's pretty exciting," she admitted.

"I'll leave you two alone then." Joseph Neely gestured to the interior of the office.

Sydney went in first, blinking to adjust her vision to the dimmer light.

Cole came in behind her and pointed to a round, mahogany meeting table.

She followed his signal and everything inside her turned still. Laid majestically out on a purple, velvet cloth, was the Thunderbolt of the North. The brooch of kings. The stuff of legends.

Sydney sucked in a breath. It was large, boldly crafted,

magnificent in every way. The polished-gold lightning bolt was scattered almost randomly with rubies, emeralds and diamonds. It was big. It was audacious. It was everything she'd ever hoped for.

She circled it, running her fingers across the soft cloth, letting them get close, but not touching the treasure. "You are one lucky man," she said in a reverent, husky voice.

His voice was equally hushed. "Sometimes I think so."

"This is the thrill of a lifetime."

"You can touch it, you know."

She rubbed her fingertips together, sensitizing them. Then she leaned in ever so slowly, resting her hips against the edge of the table.

After a long minute she dared to touch the bottom point of the brooch.

She immediately snatched her hand back, a chill creeping into her veins. She felt it again, and her world came to a screeching halt.

"Cole?" she ventured slowly, stomach clenching.

"Yeah?" He'd moved closer, but his voice seemed to come from a long way off.

She tested the bottom diamond one more time and her heart went flat, dead cold.

"This is a fake."

"Don't be absurd," said Cole, studying Sydney's shocked expression.

"It's a fake," she repeated more passionately.

"Right," Cole drawled, glancing down at the brooch. Somebody had bypassed the alarm and broken into the lawyer's safe to reproduce the Thunderbolt without anyone noticing. That was likely.

"When was it last appraised?"

Cole tried to figure out where she was going with this.

"When?" she demanded.

"It's been closely guarded for hundreds of years." The odds of it being a fake were ridiculously slim.

Had Kyle been right about her? Was this some kind of an elaborate con?

"What are you up to?" he demanded.

"I'm *up to* giving you my professional opinion."

"Uh, huh." He struggled to figure out her angle. How she could turn this little ruse to her advantage?

She pointed to the brooch. "See those diamonds? The little ones on the points?"

He glanced down. "Sure."

"They're cut."

"So what?"

"So, nobody faceted diamonds until the fourteenth century. They didn't have the tools. The process hadn't been invented. I don't know who made this brooch, but it sure wasn't the ancient Vikings."

Cole's gaze shot back to the Thunderbolt. He'd seen it dozens of times. It looked the same. It always looked the same.

But she was sounding alarmingly credible, and he couldn't for the life of him figure out how lying about its authenticity would help her get her hands on it. His stomach sank. He had to allow for the possibility that she was telling the truth.

Her voice went up an octave. "Cole, you're not reacting."

He lifted it, holding the glittering gold to the light, speaking to himself. "Who would fake it?"

"We need more information," said Sydney, squinting at the jewel. "I have a friend who's a conservator. She could pinpoint the date more closely, give us somewhere to start."

Ah. Okay. There it was. He could see the scam now.

"You have a friend," he mocked, palming the brooch.

"Gwen Parks. She's worked at the Laurent for—"

"And your *friend* is going to come out and value my brooch?"

Sydney's eyes narrowed. "She's not going to value it—"

Cole let out a chopped laugh. "Let me guess." He took a pace forward. "It'll be worthless. You'll offer to take it off my hands. And the next thing I know it'll be on display in New York."

Sydney's expression lengthened in apparent horror. "Cole, I'd never—"

"Never *what?*" He stepped closer to her again. "Never try anything and everything to get your hands on the Thunderbolt? Never lie? Never cheat? Never marry me or sleep with me?"

She clenched her hands into small fists. "I really don't give a damn what you think of me right now. But the brooch is a fake. Get my expert. Get your own expert. Take it to the Louvre. But if you don't find out *when* it was faked, you're never going to find out *why* it was faked, you are never, *ever* going to have a hope in hell of getting the real one back."

Cole stared at her in silence. Was she serious? She looked serious.

He opened his palm and inspected the brooch.

"Think about it, Cole," she stressed. "Run it through your suspicious, little mind. How could I possibly get away with it? How, in the world, could I think for one minute that I could get away *pretending* the Thunderbolt was a fake?"

Cole closed his hand again, letting the points of the brooch dig into his palm.

She was right. But who would fake it? Who *could* fake it? And who could do it so well that nobody had ever noticed?

There were no pictures of it in circulation. It would have to be somebody who had access to it for more than—

A light bulb exploded in his brain. He stomped his way to the office door, flinging it open.

"Joseph!" he bellowed.

The lawyer appeared almost immediately, bustling his way down the corridor. "Mr. Erickson?" His voice betrayed his obvious concern.

Cole stepped back into the office and closed the door for privacy. "We need an appraiser. Now."

"A conservator," said Sydney.

Both men turned to look at her.

"A museum conservator," she repeated. "One who specializes in gems and jewelry."

"Is something wrong?" asked Joseph Neely.

"The brooch has been faked," said Cole, watching the man closely. Somebody at the firm could easily be the culprit.

Neely was silent for a long moment. He didn't look guilty, but his lawyer brain was obviously clicking through the implications. When he finally spoke, his voice was a rasp. "I don't see how it could have—"

"We need to find out when and how and why," said Cole, accepting that Sydney was telling the truth.

This was a catastrophe.

His chest tightened at the thought of his grandmother's distress. He had to help her. He had to protect her.

No matter what happened, she could never find out.

In Neely's office eight hours later, the words on the newly penned conservator's report blurred in front of Cole's tired eyes. Joseph had offered the use of the facilities as long as they needed them. It was probably half generosity, half concern for the firm's liability. Cole didn't particularly care which one. He just wanted some answers.

After gauging the level of expertise at the local museum, he'd given in and flown Sydney's colleague Gwen Parks down from New York. The two women had talked technical for a couple of hours, quickly losing Cole. But it didn't matter. The only thing important to him was the final verdict.

Gwen had just confirmed that the brooch was indeed a reproduction, and that it was made sometime between nineteen fifty and nineteen seventy-five. It didn't tell them who, and it didn't tell them why, but it did tell them that they had at least a small hope of finding the real one.

"I can put out some feelers," Gwen was saying to Sydney while Joseph put the brooch back in its box to be returned to the safe.

Cole dimly wondered why he bothered. Sure the jewels themselves were valuable, but they were also replaceable. A fifty-year-old ruby, emerald and diamond reproduction was hardly something to lock up in titanium.

He clenched his fist, crumpling it around the report.

"If anybody's ever sold it, or offered it for sale..." Gwen continued, leaning against Joseph's wide mahogany desk "...somebody out there will know something."

Gwen might be dressed in blue jeans and a Mets T-shirt, but the woman had convinced Cole she knew her stuff.

"You got a way into the black market?" asked Sydney.

Gwen nodded her pixie blond head.

Both women were silent for a moment. Sydney didn't ask any questions, and Gwen didn't offer an explanation.

Sydney turned her attention to Cole. "I think we should go talk to Grandma now."

Cole jerked his head up. "What?"

"Gwen's going to try her contacts, but we need to get information from Grandma. The sooner, the better."

"We're not telling Grandma." That point was nonnegotiable.

Sydney brought her hands to her hips. "Of course we are."

Cole dropped the report on the desk. "Do you have any idea how much this will upset her?"

Sydney took a couple of paces toward him, gesturing with an open palm. "Of course it'll upset her. But never finding the Thunderbolt will upset her a whole lot more."

Cole clenched his jaw. "We'll find it without her."

"She had it during the years it was copied. She's our best lead."

"No."

"Cole. Be reasonable. She can tell us where it was, during what time periods."

"The lawyer's records will tell us that."

"All they can tell us is when it was or was not in their safe. Grandma can tell us if it was ever missing, if anybody borrowed it—"

"My answer is no."

Sydney moved directly in front of him and crossed her arms over her chest. "What makes this your decision?"

A pulse leaped to life in Cole's temple. He straightened to his full height, matching her posture. "You will *not* go behind my back and talk to my grandmother."

"The police might. A crime has been committed here, Cole."

"We'll take care of it privately." There was no way in the world Cole was losing control of the investigation, having it dumped into the lap of some overworked police precinct.

"Cole," came Gwen's voice.

Sydney and Cole both turned. Gwen straightened away from the desk, tucking her blond hair behind her ears and moving her small frame into the thick of the conversation.

"Sydney's right. No matter who you talk to, who you ask for help, public, private or otherwise, the first thing they're going to want to do is talk to your grandma. And if they don't, you should fire them for incompetence."

Sydney spoke up again. "She's our only lead."

It didn't matter. "She's seventy years old."

"She's tough as nails."

"The stress could kill her."

Sydney stared at him levelly with those penetrating green eyes. "It's not going to kill her."

They were intelligent eyes, Cole acknowledged. Clear-thinking, logical eyes. He'd never doubted she was smart. Never doubted she was capable. And this was definitely her field of expertise.

Damn.

If he wanted to keep the police out of it, he needed to keep Sydney and Gwen in, which meant he needed to take their advice.

He hated it, but there it was.

"Okay," he said. "Fine. We'll talk to Grandma."

"Tonight?" asked Sydney.

"Tomorrow," said Cole. He wasn't waking Grandma out of a sound sleep to give her bad news.

Gwen plucked her purse from the desktop. "In that case, I'd better get back to New York."

Cole quickly crossed the room and held out his hand. "Thank you very, very much for coming on such short notice." He was a lot more grateful to Gwen than he'd probably let on.

"Thanks for chartering the plane," said Gwen with a shake.

"Whatever you need," said Cole. "You just call me. Anything. Anytime."

Gwen nodded. "For now, I'll just be making phone calls. But I'll keep you guys posted." She glanced at her watch. "It'll be morning in London by the time I get home."

"You think the brooch is overseas?" asked Cole, his stomach hollowing out all over again. They were looking for a needle in a haystack.

"I'm going to check every possibility," said Gwen.

Sydney moved between them to give Gwen a hug. "Thank you," she whispered.

"Happy to help," said Gwen, glancing sideways at Cole and giving him a final once-over. "Talk to you tomorrow."

As Gwen left the office, Sydney sucked in a deep breath, blinking her exhaustion-filled eyes. But instead of complaining, she touched Cole's shoulder. His muscle instantly contracted beneath his jacket.

"We'll break it to her gently," she said.

Cole felt the weight of forty generations pressing down on him. "I don't see how we'll manage that."

Grandma greeted Sydney with a hug in the octagonal entryway. "Well? Did he do it? Did he pop the question?"

"Grandma," Cole warned.

"I hope he had a ring."

"He didn't have a ring," said Sydney.

Grandma glanced from one to the other. "But Katie said it was love at first sight. I'd hoped that was the point of this special trip."

"We are getting married," said Cole, although Sydney couldn't imagine why he bothered keeping up the charade. Katie knew their secret, and the Thunderbolt might never be found. A quickie wedding sure didn't matter anymore.

She hadn't let the full impact of that sink in yet. The odds of finding the Thunderbolt in time for the show one month away were almost nonexistent. She'd have to call it off. She'd lose her job, and her reputation would be ruined. She'd be lucky to get a position as a tour guide.

"I knew it," said Grandma, clasping her hands together. "I could tell by the way you looked at her."

"Grandma."

"Come in, come in." She backed into the living room. "I'll make tea. Tell me everything. What's the date? Where's the ceremony? Sydney, dear, you'll have to give me a guest list."

"We don't need tea. And there is no date."

"Of course we need tea. There are arrangements to make, plans to finalize. Thank goodness we already picked out the house." She took a deep breath and her grin widened.

Sydney felt sick. This should have been a happy occasion. It should have been a celebration.

"Can we please sit down?" asked Cole in a grave tone.

"Of course." Grandma gestured toward the burgundy couch. "You sit down. I'll be right back."

"Grandma." Cole's tone was sharp.

Sydney squeezed his arm, but he shook her off.

"What?" asked Grandma, blinking.

Sydney shifted between them and took Grandma's hand, trying to diffuse the building tension.

"Grandma," she said, looking into her blue eyes. She tried to let her tone give away the mood of the upcoming conversation. "We need to talk to you about something."

Grandma glanced at Cole then back to Sydney. A sly grin grew on her face. "Will it be a...quick...wedding?"

"You're not helping." Cole ground the words out from behind Sydney.

"We have some…unsettling news," said Sydney.

Grandma glanced from one to the other again. The expectant glimmer in her eyes dimmed slightly. "Oh?"

Sydney eased Grandma onto the couch. Cole crouched down in front of them and took a breath. "There's no easy way to say this," he began.

"Is someone sick?" asked Grandma, looking worried.

"No. Everybody's fine. Grandma. It's the Thunderbolt."

She stilled. After a silent heartbeat, her eyes went wide and her lips paled a shade.

"We stopped at Joseph's office," Cole continued. "The real Thunderbolt is missing. The one that's in the safe is a fake."

Grandma's hand went to her chest and her cheeks turned white as paper.

Cole jumped up. "Grandma?"

Sydney stood, too, mentally cursing herself for not taking Cole's advice. The shock really was too much for Grandma.

"Grandma?" Cole repeated.

But she still didn't answer.

"Let's lay her down," said Sydney, tossing a pillow to the far end of the couch. "Grandma? We should elevate your feet."

Cole stood back while Sydney gently repositioned her.

"I'm calling Dr. Diers," he said.

"Good idea," Sydney agreed, mentally berating herself.

Why had she thought Grandma could take this? The woman's heritage had been stolen. They should have looked for it themselves, exhausted all other possibilities. But, no, Sydney had gone for speed, and she might have harmed a wonderful woman in the process.

Grandma gripped Sydney's hand, trembling slightly. "I don't need a doctor."

"Don't try to talk," Sydney whispered.

The old woman's eyes fluttered closed. Her wrinkled skin looked frail and transparent. Her gray hair was thin, and there were age spots dotted over her forehead.

Cole hung up the phone. "Dr. Diers is on his way. How is she?"

Grandma's breathing was shallow but steady.

"I don't need a doctor," she rasped.

Cole moved forward. "Well, you're getting one anyway."

"Waste of time," said Grandma.

He crouched down and Sydney shifted out of the way. "Grandma," he said in a gentle voice, taking her hand. "We're going to find it."

Her eyes opened and she stared at him in silence for a long moment. "I know you will." And then tears formed in the corners of her eyes.

"She's resting comfortably," said Dr. Diers, quietly closing the door to Grandma's bedroom. "She's obviously had a shock."

"We gave her some bad news," said Cole, turning from the big picture window. "Probably should have kept our mouths shut."

His shoulders were tense and Sydney knew he blamed himself. But it was her fault. Trying to salvage her career on the back of an old woman was unforgivable.

"I've given her a light sedative," said Dr. Diers. "She's going to be fine. She'd like to see you."

Cole nodded and made a move toward the bedroom.

"Sydney," said the doctor.

"Yes?" asked Sydney.

"Your grandma asked to see Sydney."

Sydney straightened in surprise and Cole blinked.

"Why does she want to see Sydney?"

The doctor gave a slight shrug. "Maybe she'd rather talk to a woman?"

"I can go get Katie," he said.

"She did ask for Sydney."

"I'll go in," Sydney agreed.

Cole took a jerking step toward her.

"I promise," said Sydney, holding up her palm. "I'll just listen to what she has to say."

"I can't let you upset her," said Cole. "We've made enough mistakes already."

"I'm not going to upset her."

Cole's mouth was taut and his knuckles were white; guilt was obviously eating him up.

"We had no choice," said Sydney, trying to reassure him.

"Oh, yes, we did."

True enough. She wasn't about to take on that debate. "I'll go find out what she wants, then we can talk, okay?"

Before he could tell her no, she cut through the entrance foyer to the bedroom door, turning the cut-glass knob as quietly as possible, just in case Grandma had fallen asleep.

Grandma's eyes were open, but the sparkle was gone from their blue depths. The harsh, noonday sun streamed in through the paned window, making her look small and frail beneath the patchwork quilt.

"Sydney," she whispered, reaching for a hankie.

Sydney clicked the door shut and came to her side. "Can I get you anything? A drink of water? An aspirin?"

"I've done something terrible, Sydney," said Grandma, dabbing the hankie beneath her nose.

"Grandma?" Sydney crouched down by the bed. "What's wrong?"

"Everything's wrong."

"Tell me."

Grandma grasped Sydney's hand, searching her eyes. She drew a breath. "I have no right to ask."

"Go ahead and ask."

"What I did. What I'm going to say. Please don't tell my family."

"Of course I won't."

Grandma drew a breath, and there was a catch in her voice as her glance slid away from Sydney's. "It was me."

"What was you?"

"I faked the Thunderbolt."

A jolt of shock ricocheted through Sydney's body. "What? When? How?" Then she quickly shut her mouth, biting back more staccato questions.

She forced herself to moderate her voice. "Do you know where the real one is?"

Grandma shook her head miserably. "No."

"I don't understand," said Sydney, straining not to sound judgmental. Why on earth would Grandma fake her own heirloom? Did she need money?

"It was a long time ago."

Sydney nodded, waiting for this to start making sense.

"I was young, only twenty." Grandma's voice faded and a faraway look came into her eyes.

Sydney carefully lowered herself to the carpet, trying not to interrupt the flow of the story. She rested her back against the small bedside table, placing her hand on Grandma's.

"It was Harold's and my second anniversary, and I was pregnant with Neil. And there was this woman…"

Sydney's heart sank.

"She had a baby. A son." Grandma's voice broke. "He was six months old…"

"I'm sorry."

Grandma shook her head. "She said things. She knew things." She looked into Sydney's eyes. "I could tell it was all true."

Sydney groaned in heartfelt sympathy. What a hurtful secret. What a terrible thing for Grandma to experience. "I am *so* sorry."

"Things weren't like they are now," Grandma continued, "the neighbors would have gossiped, Neil would have been ostracized, sales from the ranch might have dropped."

"Did you talk to him?" asked Sydney. It was Harold's responsibility to make it right.

Grandma shook her head.

"Why not?"

"We'd been through so much. We'd come so far."

Sydney didn't understand.

"I was lonely that first year, and I blamed Harold, and we weren't..." The silence stretched.

"It wasn't your fault," said Sydney. Infidelity was not justifiable, no matter what was going on in a relationship.

Grandma gave a watery smile. "The Thunderbolt was all my doing." She stabbed a finger against her chest. "Me. I was young and inexperienced. Then I was afraid of what people might say. Bottom line, I wanted my husband and our life *more* than I wanted a piece of jewelry."

A cold chill snaked up Sydney's spine. "What are you saying?"

Grandma impatiently swiped at a tear with the back of her hand. "I gave it away."

Oh, no.

"She demanded the Thunderbolt and I gave it to her."

Sydney's entire body cringed.

"She said Rupert was the first-born Erickson, and so he was entitled. She promised she'd leave us alone forever."

"She blackmailed you?"

Grandma nodded, her voice quavering. "And I was a willing victim. To save my marriage, I betrayed my family."

Sydney closed her eyes. "Did it work?"

Grandma gave a short laugh. "It worked. It worked for thirty years. Except..."

Sydney dropped her head forward onto her chest. There was nothing she could say, nothing anybody could say. The Thunderbolt was gone.

In her mind she saw a flash of her mother's blond hair, the twinkle of her silver locket—the heirloom that had been snatched away from Sydney. She didn't know for sure, but she thought it was the day before the fire. She was five years old, and it was the last day her mother had held her. The last day she'd seen the silver locket, or anything else her family had ever owned.

"Can you get it back?" Grandma asked in a small voice. "Because if you could get it back..."

Sydney opened her eyes and nodded. "Yes," she promised, although she had no idea how she was going to keep it. Then a vow came from the deepest recesses of her being. "No matter who has it. No matter where it is."

Hope rose in Grandma's eyes, and a little color came back to her cheeks. "I made a mistake."

"No, you made a decision."

"How can I explain—" Grandma's voice broke. "The boys..."

"Cole and Kyle don't have to know." Sydney shook her head. "Your secret is safe with me."

Seven

"Katie?" Cole held the phone to his ear as he watched the dust billow out behind the doctor's deep-treaded SUV tires.

"Hey, Cole," his sister-in-law answered cheerfully around the whistling of a teakettle. "What's going on? Where was Sydney last night?"

"Can you come down to Grandma's right away?"

"Why?" The whistling subsided.

Cole shifted away from the closed bedroom door, dropping his voice to make sure he wasn't overheard. "Because we need you."

A beat went by before Katie spoke. "What's wrong?"

"Is Kyle there?"

"Cole, what's wrong?"

"It's not…" he began. Not what? Not bad? Not major? Not terrible?

The reality was, it was all of those things and more. He straightened the black-and-white picture of his grandfather that hung above the mantel. "Listen, I'd really rather tell you guys in person—"

The tension rose in Katie's voice. "To hell with that."

Cole gripped the carved wood fireplace mantel. "You sure Kyle's not there?"

"He's in the barn. Give!"

"Fine. Okay." Where to start? He couldn't just blurt out that the brooch was missing. "Sydney and I stayed over in Wichita Falls."

The concern in Katie's voice vanished, replaced by interest. "You did? But I thought..."

"Not for that."

"No? Because, you know, she's really a—"

"Can you just come down to Grandma's?"

"Is Sydney still with you?"

"Yes."

Katie paused and he could almost hear her smiling. "Sure. We'll be right there."

"Good." Cole squeezed his eyes shut, trying to alleviate the pounding between his temples.

The door to Grandma's bedroom squeaked open and he punched the off button on the phone.

He turned to face Sydney. "She okay?"

Sydney nodded, blinking glassy, reddened eyes, rubbing her upper arms as if the air-conditioning was too cold for her. "She's fine."

"You okay?" he asked, peering more closely. Was she upset about her career? That would be understandable.

"I'm perfect." She waved away his concern, as if it was a gnat buzzing around her head.

Okay. No sympathy. Fine. "What did Grandma say?"

"She said the brooch was at the ranch for several months in 1978."

"Does she know who faked it?"

"My best suggestion is you talk to the local people who were around back then. Maybe—"

"So, she doesn't know."

Sydney took a sharp breath, as if he was annoying her again. "Maybe you could find out who saw it, if anyone seemed to have a particular interest in it..."

Cole told himself to ignore her mood. She had to be disappointed in the turn of events. Her career was on the line, and he couldn't blame her for thinking about herself.

He nodded. Interviewing the neighbors seemed like as good a place as any to start.

Sydney turned to gaze out the front window, tugging the elastic out of her hair and finger-combing it to redo the ponytail. "While you talk to the local people, I'm going to California—"

"*California?*" Where the hell had that come from?

She nodded, still gazing at the snowcapped mountain peaks on the far side of the valley. "Gwen is, uh, sending a list of likely antique dealers. There's a concentration of them in California, and I can check—"

"Uh-uh. No way." Cole shook his head. He acknowledged that she was a valuable asset to the search, but he wasn't letting her take over completely. It was his family, his property. She simply had a passing commercial interest.

Sydney turned to face him. "What do you mean no way?"

"*I'm* going to California."

"You don't know a thing about antiques."

"If you go, I go."

"But somebody has to stay here."

"Kyle can interview the neighbors."

Sydney jerked back. "Kyle?"

"He and Katie are on their way here."

"Now?"

"Yes. Now."

Her eyes narrowed. "You told them?"

"No. But I'm about to."

"But…"

"But what?"

Sydney bit down on her lower lip, the wheels of her brain obviously churning a million miles an hour. "I just think the fewer people who know…"

"Kyle's my brother."

She got a funny look in her eyes.

Was she worried?

Afraid?

Scheming?

Would he ever be able to trust this woman again? She couldn't have predicted the brooch had been faked. But Kyle had pegged her as an opportunist. Was she trying to make this latest turn of events work for her?

"I think this'll work better if you stay here," she said, her gaze darting away from his.

"Not going to happen, Sydney."

"But—"

"Kyle can do the home front. I go with you."

"I, uh, work better alone."

He took two steps toward her. "Tough. Get used to me. Because I'm your new partner."

Cole just had to come to California.

He had to be underfoot. He couldn't have stayed home and interviewed the neighbors like a good little cowboy.

Sydney wriggled beneath the desk in her hotel room

at the Sands in Oceanside, searching for the power outlet for her rented laptop. Why did they always have the electrical plug stashed behind furniture? Did they cater to contortionists?

It took all her strength to inch the desk away from the wall. Then she yanked out the lamp cord, plugged in her converter and shimmied her way back up to the chair.

She pushed her hair off her face and shot an uneasy glance at the connecting door as she flashed up the power. The front desk had given them adjoining rooms, but she hadn't opened the door, and Cole hadn't knocked.

Right now, all she wanted was to get Gwen's e-mails downloaded. Neither Cole nor Gwen knew Grandma's secret, and handing Gwen's leads to Cole in careful sequence was the only way Sydney could get the job done.

They *were* here canvassing at antiques stores, just as she'd told him. But Oceanside was also the city where Harold's illicit lover, Irene Cowan, had once lived.

As soon as Sydney ditched Cole, she was heading two blocks down to city hall to take a look at the historical property records. The new tax rolls were online, but Irene Cowan wasn't a current property owner. So if a trail existed in property records, it was going to start on microfiche.

While the blue bar edged its way along the bottom of her computer screen, a knock sounded on the adjoining door. Sydney stood up, silently urging the e-mail download to hurry.

Cole knocked again.

The word "complete" came up, and Sydney snapped the lid on her laptop before crossing the room.

Cole stood in the doorway in a crisp, white shirt, a burgundy tie and a beautifully cut charcoal suit with polished, black shoes. He was freshly shaved and his hair was neatly combed. If the clerks in the antique stores were female, Sydney was pretty sure they had a shot at getting information from them.

"I thought we'd get more cooperation if we looked like big buyers," he said.

Big buyers nothing, the staff would be too busy flirting with Cole to care whether or not they'd make a sale.

Sydney glanced down at her black jeans and the cropped, lacy top that was streaked with dust from her foray under the desk. She was definitely outclassed.

She opened the closet and took an ivory suit in one hand and a little black dress in the other. "Professional or flirtatious?" she asked.

His gaze moved back and forth. "What usually works best for you?"

"Professional," she said. Then she paused. "No. I'm lying." She hung the suit back up and closed the closet. "Flirtatious wins hands down." She rounded the privacy wall to the powder room.

Cole laughed behind her. "I know it would work on me."

"Yeah? Well, you're easy."

"So is most of the male population of this country."

"There's a list of antique stores on the desk," she called, bailing on this conversation before it went bad.

She wiggled out of her jeans and peeled off her blouse, turfing the white bra that would show at her shoulders. "I thought we'd start on Zircon Drive," she called.

"Does Gwen think one of these dealers has seen the Thunderbolt?" he asked in return.

"Nothing specific so far." Sydney ran a brush through her hair and dug into her makeup bag.

"So, what exactly are we doing here?"

"We take the picture of the fake around to the employees and see if they recognize it."

"And if they don't?"

His voice was closer, and Sydney quickly glanced around for the dress. Not that she was afraid he'd come in. He was way too much of a gentleman for that. It was more that his voice and her naked body were a potent combination.

She slipped the dress over her head, the silky fabric teasing her breasts on the way down.

"Sydney?"

"Then we move on to the next store," she said in a voice that was more than a little husky.

Cole was silent for a moment. "You really think this is going to work?"

"I don't know," she answered honestly.

"You almost ready?"

"Just putting on my shoes." She brushed her hair one more time and popped a pair of diamond studs into her ears before heading out to meet him.

His gaze strayed up and down her clingy outfit. His expression gave away nothing, but her skin prickled as if he actually touched her.

"We should go," she said, forcing her thoughts to the search instead of her hormones.

Cole stared at her a minute longer. Then he cleared his throat. "Right. Zircon Drive." He abruptly turned and headed for the door.

"This is ridiculous," said Cole as they exited from the fourth Oceanside antique store. Despite Sydney's cleavage and Cole's sexy baritone, none of the staff admitted having seen or heard of the Thunderbolt.

"We've barely started," Sydney countered, knowing that no matter what they wore or what they promised, their odds of finding information were almost nil. She was feeling guiltier by the hour for keeping him in the dark about the real search.

"We could blow off a year like this," he said.

"You and I are only one part of the investigation," she argued. "Gwen is checking Europe, and Kyle is interviewing your neighbors."

"While you and I are wasting time."

Sydney skirted around a group of teenage boys who strutted three-wide on the sidewalk in the opposite direction. She hop-stepped in her high heels to catch up to Cole. "Give it a chance."

"We need more manpower," he said as the oncoming crowd parted around him. "I'm hiring a P.I. firm. Somebody national, with lots of investigators."

She ducked in behind him, following in his wake as she fought a spurt of panic. A dozen private eyes? Sticking their noses into the investigation? They'd make it impossible to keep Grandma's secret.

"Let's wait and see instead," she suggested.

"Wait and see what?"

The crowds thinned and she moved back to his side. "Wait and see what Gwen comes up with."

He peered down his nose at her, obviously unconvinced.

"Before we do anything rash," she elaborated. "Okay?"

"Hiring a P.I. firm is *rash?*"

"I think we need to focus our effort."

He turned his palms up, fingers spread wide in a gesture of incredulity. His voice rose as they angled toward the curb. "There's nothing to focus *on.*"

"You're so impatient."

Cole glared his frustration while he unlocked the passenger door. "Impatient? Excuse me, but the Thunderbolt is worth half a million dollars."

Sydney folded herself into the passenger seat, adjusting her dress on the hot leather as Cole clicked the door shut.

She hadn't quantified it from the money angle yet. But the real Thunderbolt represented one of the first documented uses of diamonds as ornamentation in Europe, and the jewels themselves were dozens of carats. It was impossible to put a price on that.

Cole dropped into the driver's side and slammed the door. He cranked the engine and turned the air-conditioning up to full. "For half a million dollars, I think I can be forgiven for a little impatience."

"Fine. You're forgiven."

"And we hire a firm."

"No. Not now. Not yet."

Sydney's cell phone rang.

She could feel Cole working up a counter argument as she hunted through her purse. She hoped it was Gwen with something, *anything*. They needed a bogus lead or a false rumor to distract Cole.

She pushed the talk button. "Yes?"

"Well, well, well," Bradley Slander drawled through the grainy speaker. "You've been holding out on me, babe."

Sydney stilled, cursing under her breath, eliciting a look of surprise from Cole.

"I'm not your babe, Slander." Her voice grated into the mouthpiece as she turned toward the passenger door in a vain attempt to keep the conversation private.

"The Thunderbolt of the North?" Bradley continued. "That's big even for us."

She flicked her hair back from her sweaty forehead.

"There *is* no us." How had he found out so fast? Who did he bribe?

"Oh, there's an us, Sydney," said Bradley. "We're inextricably connected, both cosmically and financially."

"Get over yourself."

"Where are you?"

She glanced back at Cole. He was watching her intently, his hand poised on the stick shift.

"None of your business," she said.

"Gwen's bush league, Sydney," said Bradley.

"Gwen is brilliant."

"What's she found for you so far?"

Sydney clamped her jaw. She wasn't giving Bradley a thing. Not a damn thing.

"Thought so," said Bradley with a self-satisfied chuckle. "Team up with me. I know everybody who's anybody from here to Istanbul."

"Do the words 'cold day in hell' mean anything to you?"

His voice dropped to that reptilian level. "Together, babe, you and I can—"

She straightened, no longer caring if Cole or anyone else was listening. "Get this through your thick skull, Bradley. I will *not* work with you."

"Sure you will," he purred.

"No."

"You know it's just a matter of time."

"Not now. Not ever—"

Cole snagged the phone from between her fingers.

"I think you heard the lady," he said to Bradley.

Her jaw went slack in amazement.

"Really?" asked Cole mildly, his gaze drifting to Sydney. "Well, I doubt very much you know who you're messing with, either."

Then he took the phone from his ear and snapped it shut. He plopped it back into her palm. "Who *was* that?"

"Bradley Slander," she answered, staring at the compact phone, trying to decide whether he was being gentlemanly or controlling. In the end, she decided he was just being Cole. Which was…nice.

She had to admit, she'd experienced a momentary thrill when she pictured Bradley's expression. But now she was thinking about the possible ramifications. Bradley was unpredictable, and they'd just waved a red flag in his face.

"Old boyfriend?" asked Cole, still watching her closely.

She shuddered at the very thought. "Antiquity snake. Now *there's* a guy with contacts in the black market."

"But you're not willing to work with him?"

"I'd rather be dragged naked through an anthill."

Cole quirked a half smile. "Thanks for the visual."

She fought a grin, the tension finally dissipating. She was letting herself get paranoid here. Nothing terrible was going to happen. Bradley was far way, and he didn't have a clue about Grandma's secret.

"So what did he want?" asked Cole.

"He's after the Thunderbolt."

Cole's hand tightened on the shift. "Why? It's mine."

"Possession is nine-tenths of the law."

"That would make him a thief."

"I know." Sydney closed her eyes for a brief second. If Irene Cowan had sold it or given it away, especially if it was overseas, the ownership issue was going to get complicated.

"We need to find it before he does," she said. "Keeps our life simple."

Cole's stare raked over her for a silent moment. "There's something you're not telling me."

She tried not to flinch. She couldn't let him see her fear. "There are plenty of things I'm not telling you," she said, going on the offensive. "But I *am* doing everything in my power to find your brooch. I won't lie to you, if the brooch is already on the black market, Bradley's a threat."

"How big of a threat?"

"He's after it. But we've got Gwen. And Gwen is good."

Cole's expression turned speculative. "What about you, Sydney?"

"What about me?"

"Are you good?"

"At finding antiquities? I'm very good."

He nodded toward the antique store they'd just left. "So why does this feel like amateur hour?"

She struggled to keep from squirming under his gaze. "Because we haven't gotten started yet."

"Then let's get started."

Sydney nodded. "Right." She'd get the real search under way the very minute she ditched Cole.

He put the car into first gear and checked his side mirror. "Let's start with what Bradley is to you."

"A thorn in my ass."

Cole grinned, and another layer of tension dissipated.

"Ever slept with him?" asked Cole conversationally as he pulled into traffic.

"No!" She folded her arms across her chest. "And, by the way, that's none of your business."

"Sure it's my business."

"Why? Because we—" She stopped herself short.

"Because I want to know how deep this guy's vendetta goes."

Sydney puzzled over that one. "Would it be better if I'd slept with him, or worse?"

"A scorned lover makes a powerful enemy." He stopped at a red light.

She hesitated, then asked softly, "Are you my enemy, Cole?"

He turned his head. "Have I been scorned?"

She immediately realized her mistake. Reminding him of their lovemaking was a stupid idea. She cringed. "Sorry."

"For what?"

"Bringing it up."

The light changed and he pulled ahead. "What? You thought I'd forget?"

"This conversation is a bad idea."

He flipped on his signal and took a right turn. They accelerated past a sandy beach lined with palm trees and colorful umbrellas.

"Sydney," he said, keeping his attention fixed on the straight road. "Since you were there." He shifted to third. "And I was there." He pulled it into fourth. "And since we both have pretty damn good memories." He climbed on the brake pedal and swerved around a minivan exiting a parking stall. "I don't think it matters much whether we have this conversation or not."

She gripped the door handle. He made a good point. She remembered everything in vivid detail. Everything.

"We had sex," he said bluntly. "And that's that."

She pictured him mentally brushing his hands together. He was done with the subject and done with her.

Her stupid chest contracted. "Okay."

He was silent for a split second. "No hard feelings?"

"No hard feelings." None at all.

Eight

It took Sydney the entire next morning to convince Cole they needed to split up. But she finally sent him to some antique dealers across town, freeing her up to walk to city hall.

Hunched over a microfiche reader in the bowels of the building's basement, she discovered Irene Cowan had paid taxes on a little house at Risotto Beach for ten years running. But Irene's trail disappeared in the early eighties. She could have started renting, or she might have moved away.

Sydney moved on to utility records. But she found nothing new. Then, two hours later, just when she was sure she'd hit a dead end, it occurred to her to check marriage licenses.

She moved to the State offices upstairs. There, finally, she had another lead. Irene Cowan had become Irene Robertson. She and her husband had paid taxes in Oceanside for a further fifteen years. Then they'd died in a car accident in the mid-nineties.

But they'd raised one son, Rupert Cowan. And according to the Oceanside *Gazette,* he'd graduated from Edison High School and won a small scholarship to Southwestern State Fashion Design College. The Southwestern State alumni newsletter revealed that he'd received his degree then taken a job in New York.

Then Google picked up a local fashion show from last year in Miami. Rupert Cowan's company, Zap, had been a contributing designer.

It was a break. A huge break.

Rupert could be in Miami.

Sydney needed to get there just as soon as possible. She began formulating a plan. She'd approach him the way she approached any other potential seller. Not on the phone, not with a letter, but in person. She needed to see his expression, gauge his mood, his interests, his weaknesses.

This was the most important antiquity purchase she'd ever make. She was doing it step by careful step.

Her heels clicked on the floor of the cavernous, marble foyer while she dialed Gwen's number.

"Hello?" Gwen answered.

"I need you to send us to Miami."

"Sydney?"

"Yeah. It's me."

"What's in Miami?"

"I can't explain, but you need to give us some kind of a lead for Miami."

"Whoa. A false lead?"

"Yes."

"What's going on?"

"You know I wouldn't ask if it wasn't important."

"You've got something. What've you got?"

"I've got a name," Sydney admitted.

"Who? Where? How?"

"I can't tell you that. It would give away a confidence."

"You have someone else working on this?"

"It's, ah, complicated."

"I'm reasonably intelligent."

"I know." But Sydney couldn't tell Gwen. She couldn't tell anybody Rupert's name. She'd given her word to Grandma.

"So, what exactly is it that I'm doing here?"

"You're sending us to Miami."

Gwen's tone hardened. "That's not what I meant."

Sydney sighed, not sure how to answer.

"So, what? I'm window decoration?"

"Right now. Yeah."

Gwen's voice rose, her exasperation coming through loud and clear. "You mean I can stop *calling in favors* from Edinburgh to Rome?"

"Yes."

"Sydney!"

"I didn't know until this very minute. I swear, I just found out—"

"Fine."

Sydney felt like crud. "I'm sorry."

Gwen's voice was flat. "Call me if you need help."

"I will. And, Gwen?"

"Yeah?"

"I'll tell you what I can later. But this is important."

"I hear you."

"I'll call you from Miami."

"I'll be asleep." Gwen disconnected.

Sydney snapped the phone shut and pushed open the glass door.

Out on the wide, concrete staircase, she swore under her

breath. Gwen was a good friend, and a consummate professional. Maybe it would be safe to tell her…

Sydney trotted down the steps, rubbing her thumb over the keypad of her phone, trying to decide how much she could afford to tell Gwen. As she ran through the facts, Grandma's stricken expression flashed through her mind. Sydney heard her own heartfelt vow, and remembered her determination to do right by the woman.

Good friend or no good friend, she knew she'd take the secret to her grave.

"I gotta ask myself…" came a familiar, mocking voice.

Sydney blinked the world back into focus and stared directly into the face of Bradley Slander.

"…what does the Oceanside City Hall have to do with our little search?"

A cold wave of fear momentarily paralyzed her.

"This is the best one yet, Sydney." He chuckled. "Come on, tell ol' Bradley what you've got."

"Nothing." She gripped her phone, cursing herself as she increased her pace in an effort to get him away from the building.

She frantically cataloged her movements over the past few hours. Had she covered her tracks? Would the clerks remember her? Had she written anything down? Tossed evidence in the wastebasket?

How could she have been so careless as to let Bradley sneak up on her? He could have overheard her phone call to Gwen. He might already know about Miami.

"We can go fifty-fifty," he said, pacing along beside her.

"Get lost."

"Now, that's just rude."

Sydney stopped on the sidewalk and turned to stare at him, a horrible thought crossing her mind. What if he'd talked to Cole's grandmother? What if he'd gone to the ranch, lied about who he was and pumped the family for information.

"If you're so damn good, why do you need me anyway?" she asked, fishing to see how much he knew.

He moved in closer. "Because we're a *team,* Wainsbrook. It wouldn't be near as much fun without you."

"You mean, you don't want the entire profit?"

His beady eyes narrowed. "Yeah, right. You don't think for one minute I'm going to find it."

"Frankly," said Sydney, with what she hoped was an unconcerned toss of her hair, "I don't think either of us is going to find it."

"They why are you wasting your time?"

"It's my time to waste."

"What've you got?"

"I've got a missing brooch." She waited, hoping his ego would force him to give out his own information.

"We know the age of the fake," he said.

"Of course we do." She waited again.

"We know it's the Erickson family."

Sydney nodded, concentrating on keeping her expression neutral. Had he talked to Grandma? Had he been to Texas?

"You talked to them?" asked Bradley.

"I've got Cole Erickson with me now," she admitted. Maybe if she focused on Cole, Bradley wouldn't realize Grandma was of any significance.

If Bradley was surprised that she volunteered Cole's name, he didn't show it. He probably chalked it up to his superior interrogation techniques, thinking he had her right where he wanted her.

"He the guy on the phone?" Bradley asked.

"Yeah." Sydney gave a long sigh, trying to appear tired

and vulnerable. "He hasn't given me anything. You want to give him a try?"

This time, Bradley did eye her with suspicion.

She hoped she hadn't overplayed her hand.

Then he grinned, reaching out to touch the bottom of her chin. "Not."

Relief shuddered through Sydney. By sheer force of will, she didn't brush his hand away. Instead she raised her eyebrows in a question.

"Don't want to make him nervous." Bradley chuckled. "I think he's got the hots for you. Not a good idea to bring him face-to-face with his competition."

She nearly choked on that one.

Bradley moved in closer, dropping his voice to an intimate level. "Why don't *you* talk to him? I can come up with a few questions for you, and you can tell me what he says, hmm?"

Sure didn't take much for the man to think they'd joined forces. "Okay." Sydney agreed with a nod. If Bradley focused on interrogation questions for Cole, he might just stay out of city hall wastepaper baskets.

Bradley snaked an arm around her waist and she forced herself to remain still.

"Don't be afraid to get persuasive," he whispered, his hot breath irritating her skin.

What? She was supposed to break Cole's legs?

"You know what I mean." Bradley rubbed his knuckles up and down her arm. "Flirt a little. Give a little."

Sydney tightened her jaw and swallowed hard against her scathing retort. "Right," she said instead.

"That's my girl." He gave her a kiss on the cheek.

Cole watched with disbelief as an overpolished, ridiculously urbane-looking man kissed Sydney right there on the sidewalk. He gripped the steering wheel and everything inside him clenched to stone. He reached for the door handle, intent on ripping the jerk's head off, but a horn sounded behind him.

He looked up to see the light had turned green. Then he glanced back at Sydney. She was smiling at the man, their posture intimate and telling. Cole's nostrils flared and he stuffed the transmission into First.

No wonder she'd been so anxious to get rid of him this morning. She had something going on the side, and he was in the way. Whether this guy was a lover or a secret contact, her interests obviously weren't those of the Erickson family.

Cole wasn't about to sit still for that. Miss New York's plotting days were over. He was taking over as of right now. He was calling up the best PI firm in the country and putting them on retainer until the job was complete. Sydney could get the hell out of his way.

He pulled into the hotel underground and parked the car. Then he grabbed an express elevator and stomped his way down the hallway. He'd call Kyle, see if his brother had come up with any leads from the neighbors. Then he'd call Joseph Neely and get some PI firm recommendations.

Kyle didn't have any new information, so Cole moved on to Neely. Five minutes later he was armed with a list of the top-ten firms.

"Cole?" Sydney's voice wafted through the connecting doorway.

He picked up the phone, planning to start with the L.A. firm.

Her footsteps sounded on the carpet behind him. "You find any… What are you doing?"

He turned to look at her lying, cheating, beautiful face. "Better question is, what are *you* doing?"

She glanced from him to the phone and back again. "I'm looking for the Thunderbolt."

"Find it?"

"Uh...no."

"Find anything new today?"

She shook her head.

"Nothing at all? Nothing interesting?"

"Cole?"

That was it. She'd blown her last chance.

"I'm calling P.I. firms," he said, punching in the last few numbers.

She took a step forward, but something in his expression made her hesitate. Smart woman.

"Why?" she asked.

"Amber and Associates," came the voice on the telephone.

"I'm interested in hiring a private investigator," said Cole. "I need to find some missing jewelry."

Sydney moved around the bed, stopping directly in front of him. "Don't."

He ignored her.

She shot a telltale glance at the disconnect button.

He covered the mouthpiece. "Don't even think about it."

"I'll put you through to Dean Skye," said the receptionist.

"Thank you," said Cole, warning Sydney with his eyes.

"Hang up," she insisted.

"No."

"Why are you doing this?"

"So I can find the Thunderbolt."

"We *are* finding the Thunderbolt."

Cole scoffed out a sound of disbelief.

"Cole!"

"Dean Skye speaking."

"Mr. Skye," said Cole, ignoring Sydney. "I have a situation involving—"

Sydney's hand shot out.

Cole grabbed her wrist. But he was too late. The line went dead.

He squeezed. "What the—"

She winced and he immediately let her go.

"What the hell do you *think you're doing?*" he bellowed, slamming down the receiver.

"You can't do this."

"Yes. As a matter of fact, I *can.* It's my brooch. It's my problem. You don't even need to be here."

"But—"

"You're dead weight, Sydney. Go home."

She blinked. "I don't understand. What happened?"

He'd seen her in the arms of another man. That's what happened.

And he knew in that instant that he couldn't trust her. He also knew she was under his skin. He'd spent one single night in her arms, but there was no denying the acid spray of jealousy that burned through his body.

He was making decisions on emotion here. He had to send her away before he did something really stupid and compromised his family.

"Cole?"

"I know your little secret." He spat the words out.

All the color drained from her face. Her green eyes went wide, and her arms went slack by her side. "How…"

Well, if there was any doubt at all left over, *that* reaction sure confirmed that he'd seen what he'd thought he'd seen.

Cole sneered. "I saw you kissing him. Hugging him—"

"Who?"

"The guy on the sidewalk."

"Just now?"

What the hell kind of a question was that? "Yes, just now. How many guys did you kiss today?"

"You mean Bradley?"

"I don't know his name."

The color was coming back to her face. Now she looked more confused than scared. "You called in a P.I. firm because you saw Bradley Slander kiss me?"

"I called in a P.I. firm because you spent the afternoon with *Bradley* instead of doing your job."

"I was with him for two minutes."

Cole snorted. "That must have been disappointing. And, by the way, if that was Bradley Slander, he sure hasn't been scorned yet."

"You think I was having *sex with him?*" Her question ended in an incredulous shout. Then silence took over the room and she stared at him with impressive indignation.

Okay, if her reaction was anything to go by at this point…

"You kissed him goodbye," said Cole.

She paced across the room. "*He* kissed *me*. On the cheek. In public."

"You didn't exactly slap his face."

"I didn't exactly kiss him back, either. He's smart, and he's unpredictable. I just wanted him to go away."

"I saw what I saw," Cole insisted, but his voice was losing conviction.

"You saw him kiss me on the cheek, because that was all he did."

"You didn't have to smile."

"I was gritting my teeth."

Cole swallowed, allowing that he might not have connected the dots in precisely the right formation.

"Cole, I spent the afternoon researching the Thunderbolt. And I'd slit my wrists before I'd sleep with that man."

Something relaxed inside Cole. Bad sign, he knew. But there was nothing he could do about it.

Her eyes burned an emerald fire as she moved closer. "And I'm insulted that you jumped to that conclusion. Just because I slept with you—"

"I'm sorry."

"—doesn't make me—"

"I'm sorry."

She took a breath. "You're a cad, you know that?"

He nodded. "I'm a cad."

She poked him in the chest with her index finger. "You ought to be ashamed of yourself."

He nodded again. "I am."

She poked him, and this time he captured her hand.

She looked up into his eyes and her voice softened. "I'm a very reliable person. I could get references."

"I don't need references," he whispered.

She searched his expression. "Then what do you need?"

What did he need? He needed to be sure that emotion wasn't overriding reason when it came to her. He needed to know she was on his side. He needed to know she didn't have an ulterior motive.

She sighed into the silence. "Once, just *once,* do you think you could give me the benefit of the doubt?"

"Yeah," he answered. "I will."

"Good."

He inhaled the scent of her hair and something primal rose up inside him. She might not have been interested in Slander, but Slander was sure as hell interested in her. Cole felt an overpowering need to stamp out the other man's taint.

He needed to hold her, to kiss her, to remind himself that *he* was the one she'd made love with. It might be an overreaction, but the blood of pillaging Vikings pounded through his veins. Ericksons took what they wanted, and Cole wanted Sydney.

He wanted her bad.

He bent his head, bringing his lips down onto hers. He forced himself to keep his arms by his sides. She could step away if she wanted. He wasn't holding her, but he wasn't holding back, either. He was going to kiss her until she told him to stop.

But she didn't step away, and passion crested within him. His hands went to her hair. How he'd missed its satiny texture. He cradled her head, taking a small step forward, his body coming up against hers, her heat flaring against his skin.

"I missed you," he whispered, the words almost painful. "I missed you so much."

Had it only been a week since they'd made love? It seemed like an eternity.

"I missed you, too," she sighed, her soft body snuggling into the hollows of his own. "I know you're marrying someone else…"

"And I know this is just business for you…"

Their kiss deepened. He wished he could absorb her, keep her, bind her so tight she'd never touch another man. Never look at another man.

He plucked at the buttons of her blouse, needing to feel her satin skin once more.

Her blouse fell open and his fingertips skimmed their way over her stomach.

He covered one lacy cup, filling his hand with the weight of her breast. Her nipple poked into his palm and he wanted to rip off her clothes then and there. She wasn't going near another man. Ever. *Ever!*

He didn't care that it was only business. His hand convulsed around her breast, and the other went to her buttocks, dragging her tight against his body, leaving no question about the strength of his desire.

"Cole," she moaned, her body going lax.

He wrapped an arm around her waist, supporting her slight weight.

"What you do…" she groaned.

"What *you* do," he muttered back.

She wound her arms around his neck, holding him tight, her lips searing his skin.

"Cole, please," she gasped.

"Anything," he said. "Anything."

"We have to go."

"Huh?"

She stopped kissing, released him, her breath coming in short gasps. "We have to go to Miami."

Cole felt as though he'd been bucked off and hit the dirt sideways. "What?"

"I found out… Gwen called… We need to go to Miami."

He stared down at her open blouse, her lacy bra, the creamy breasts that mounded up like ambrosia. *"Now?"*

"Now. Bradley's here. We can't waste any time."

Cole pulled back, irrational anger bubbling up at the mere mention of Bradley's name. "Is that what you call this? A *waste of time?"*

She closed her eyes and let out an exasperated sigh. "Don't."

Fine. Forget it. They'd drop everything and fly across the country to play hurry up and wait. "Sure, we'll go to Miami."

"You think I *want* to stop?"

"Just say it—you're stopping, aren't you."

She tightened her jaw, bringing her hands up to her hips. "Cole Nathaniel—"

He froze at the intimate sound of his middle name.

"—I want you more than I've ever wanted any man in my life. And if I had my way—"

"You want me?"

"Yes."

"But we're leaving?"

"Yes! Bradley's going to stake out the hotel."

"But, you definitely want me." Suddenly life didn't seem so bleak. Miami was only four hours away. They could be there before morning. Nothing to do before the antique stores opened up…

She shook her head. "Yes, I want you. Should I make up a sign or something?"

"And you'll still want me in Miami?" He'd take it in writing if she'd give it to him.

"Not if you don't shut up."

Cole grinned. "Shutting up now."

"Good. Grab your bag."

"Should I call a cab?"

"No. Let's duck out the back way and catch one a few blocks down."

He gave her a squeeze. "It's sexy when you go all secret agent on me."

She shot him a look of impatience. "Want meter is going down."

"Shutting up again."

"Good thinking."

Nine

The minute the door swung shut on their Miami hotel suite, Cole pulled Sydney into his arms. Passion burst to life inside her, and she fumbled with the buttons at his collar, loosening his tie while he shucked his jacket.

She moaned her satisfaction, burrowing her face into his neck, inhaling deeply. She didn't know what it was about his scent, but if they could bottle it, they'd make a fortune. She flicked her tongue out to taste his skin, then she suckled a tender spot near his collarbone.

"You make me crazy," he rasped, running his hands through her hair.

She started on the buttons of his shirt. "You just make me want you."

"How is it I do that?"

"Breathing," she answered.

He returned her kisses, reaching for her blouse, popping

the buttons and peeling it off her shoulders. He stood back and gazed once more at her lacy bra. "I like it when you breathe, too."

She unsnapped the hooks and dropped the wisp of fabric to the floor. His eyes darkened, and her body began to hum in earnest.

"Oh, man." He slowly pulled her in, pressing them skin to skin, holding her tight and setting off tiny explosions in her brain. His hands worked magic. His kisses grew harder, sweeter, ranging further and further.

She tangled her hands in his hair, loving the touch, loving the texture. "Stop time again," she begged.

He feathered his fingertips down her spine. "I'll do my best." He tasted her earlobe. He kissed her neck. He delved sweetly into her mouth, and she thought she never wanted him to stop.

How had she imagined she could live without this?

They'd wasted six whole days, avoiding each other when they could have been in paradise. It was almost criminal.

He peeled off the rest of their clothes, and his touch grew more intimate. A flush covered her body, and an overhead fan whirred a gentle breeze, cooling the heat, sensitizing her skin.

He scooped her into his arms once again and crossed through the French doors to the king-size bed.

"Tell me when to put you down," he said.

A shudder ran through her at his selfless memory. "Not yet."

She loved this. There was something about his strength, his caring, his bold masculinity that sent shivers to her core.

He smiled and kissed her lips. Then he kissed her eyelids and the tip of her nose. "You really like this," he teased.

"I really like this," she agreed.

"Gotta figure out what fantasy it is."

She grinned. "Caveman?"

"Viking."

Her body convulsed. "That's it."

His eyes turned stormy. And he sobered, covering her lips in a long, deep kiss as he gently laid her back on the bed. He brushed her hair from her eyes. "You're beautiful."

She felt beautiful. She felt desirable and wonderful.

He kissed his way up her body beginning with her ankle, then the bend of her knee, gently flexing her leg until he had access to her inner thigh. His days growth of beard gently abraded her tender skin, sending shivers of desire to her core. His lips nibbled and his tongue teased higher and higher while she gasped his name.

She tensed when he blew gently on her curls. But then she closed her eyes and bit down on her lip as sensation after sensation throbbed their way along her limbs.

This was Cole. She was safe. He wouldn't hurt her. He wouldn't hurt anyone.

Then his hand replaced his mouth, gently stretching and filling her as he moved on to kiss her stomach. Her hips came off the bed, and he murmured words of encouragement against her skin.

She grasped for his hair, her hands restless, needing something to do. He moved again and took one nipple into his mouth. She groaned, burying her fingers in his hair. Her entire body arched involuntarily, striving to get closer to the sensations that were driving her sweetly out of her mind.

She dug her fingernails into his shoulders, raking them down his back as he moved up to kiss her mouth.

She opened wide. Finally, finally. She wrapped her arms around his broad body, holding him tight against her breasts. She kissed his mouth, kissed his cheeks, kissed his eyelids, then buried her face in his neck and inhaled.

He kissed the top of her head, one hand stroking down her glistening body, coming to rest on her bottom. "Slow and you just don't go together, do they?" he gasped.

"Get over it, cowboy," she rumbled, reveling in the salty taste of his neck.

She felt his deep chuckle.

"I'll try," he promised, easing her thighs apart. "I'll try really, really hard."

He eased inside her inch by careful inch. She bit down hard on her bottom lip. Time was stopping again.

He did slow it down. Then he sped it up. Then slowed it down again, holding her shimmering until she was sure she'd cry out in desperation. He whispered her name over and over, until the city lights blurred and streamed together, melting into the hot, humid ground.

Hours later, the rising sun turned the edge of the ocean a pearly pink. The champagne bottle was three quarters empty. And the lazy ceiling fan pushed a breeze down on Cole's bare skin.

He dipped a fresh strawberry into the bowl of whipped cream on the bedside table and held it to Sydney's lips.

She bit down, smiling her appreciation of the delicacy.

He popped the other half into his own mouth, thinking he could happily stay here for the rest of his life.

"So," she continued around the berry. "Your great-great-granddaddy, the infamous and sexy Jarred Erickson—"

"I believe I take after him," said Cole, pushing himself into a sitting position, striking a pose among half a dozen plump, white pillows and a billowing comforter.

"The sexy part or the infamous part?" she asked, bend-ing her knees to cross her ankles in the air and resting her chin on her interlaced fingers.

Cole took in her tousled hair and her bare buttocks. Yep. Definitely forever. "I'm thinking both," he said.

She grinned and reached for her champagne flute. "So you're telling me Jarred decreed that the ranch should stay as one parcel into perpetuity?"

Cole nodded. "My ancestors were big on decrees. Every few generations, somebody comes up with something that wreaks havoc for a couple hundred years."

He figured most of them were lunatics, particularly those who had taken to piracy.

She took a sip of the champagne, and he had to curb an urge to kiss the sweetness from her mouth.

"And your solution is to come up with some new decrees?" she asked.

"Damn straight. It's my turn. I complied with theirs—"

Sydney coughed out a laugh.

"What?"

"You complied with *what,* exactly?"

"Passing on the Thunderbolt."

"Ha. You had to be railroaded into marriage."

That was unfair. He frowned at her. "It's completely voluntary."

"As a last resort."

He reached for his own champagne, leaning back against the birch headboard. "Point is, it'll get the job done."

"You're also splitting the ranch in half, in defiance of Great-great-granddaddy Jarred."

"That's just common sense. Keeping it intact was a stupid idea."

"Are you always this determined that you're right and everyone else is wrong?"

"Of course."

"Of course," she mimicked.

"Hey, if a man doesn't trust his own judgment, what's left?"

She laughed again, nearly spilling her champagne. Then she twisted into a sitting position, rearranging the comforter over her lap. "You know, whoever came up with the wenches and ale rule, sure had you Erickson men pegged."

"Wenches and ale?"

"Yeah. You know. The wenches and ale."

"I have no idea what you're talking about."

"Didn't your grandma tell you?"

Cole shook his head.

Sydney leaned across him, snagging another strawberry and dipping it in the cream. "That's why the women get the brooch." She popped the berry into her mouth. "Somebody back in the fourteenth century decided you guys might sell it for wenches and ale. You know, the Erickson of the day would change the tradition. And, poof, there would go the Thunderbolt."

Cole couldn't help but grin.

"What?" she asked.

"Who needs wenches and ale?" He lifted his flute in a mock toast. "I've got champagne and—"

"Watch it, cowboy."

He leaned forward and kissed her strawberry lips, taking the safe route. "A princess."

She pulled back. "A *princess?*"

Okay, too sappy. "A hot babe?"

She raised her eyebrows.

He decided to go with the truth. "A beautiful, intelligent, funny, gracious lady?"

"That's not bad."

He took the champagne from her hand and set both glasses down on the bedside table. "Come here," he said, needing to feel her all over again. He gathered her into his arms and they stretched out on the comforter.

She sighed and rested her head on his shoulder.

He stroked her hair, releasing its scent. "Wenches and ale. How is it you know more about my family than I do?"

"I'm nosey. I ask lots of questions."

He settled his arm more comfortably around her. Traffic sounds came to life on the street below, and the rising sun flashed its orange rays through the balcony doors.

"Let me ask *you* a question," he said, twirling a lock of her hair around his index finger.

"Fire away."

"You said you had foster parents."

She nodded. "I lost my parents in a house fire when I was five."

Cole tightened his arm around her, and the ceiling fan whooshed into the silence.

"My foster parents were friends of the family. Nanny Emma and Papa Hal raised me. But they were older. And they've both since passed away."

Cole's heart went out to her. He didn't know what he'd do without his family. "You must miss them all."

"Nanny and Papa, yes. But I don't really remember my parents at all. I have these vague images of them in my mind."

"What about pictures?"

"Burned in the fire. A few of the neighbors had shots of my father from a distance, but they tell me my mother was always behind the camera, not in front of it."

Cole's chest tightened at the injustice. Never to know what your mother looked like? At twenty, he'd ached for his mother. Sydney had been five.

Protective instincts welled up inside him. "What about newspapers? Her high school yearbook? Surely somebody—"

"It's okay." Sydney reached over and stroked her palm across his beard-stubbled cheek, comforting him, when he should have done it for her.

"What *do* you remember?" he asked, covering her small hand with his own.

"My mother's locket." Sydney relaxed against him again, smiling at what was obviously a touchstone memory. "It was silver, oval-shaped. It had a flower, I think it was a rose, etched into the front. I don't know whose picture was inside, but it would dangle down when she bent over to hug me. I distinctly remember reaching for it. Her hair was blond, and it sort of haloed around the locket."

"Where's the locket now?"

"Destroyed by the fire."

"Oh, Sydney."

"It's really okay."

He tucked her hair behind one ear and gently kissed the top of her head. "I guess that explains a lot."

She tipped her chin to look up at him, green eyes narrowing. "Explains what?"

"Your profession. Your burning desire to locate antiquities."

She pulled back. "I locate antiquities because I have a master's degree in art history."

"You have a master's degree because you've spent your life looking for the locket."

"That's silly. The locket was destroyed more than twenty years ago."

He touched her temple with his index finger. "Maybe in here." He placed his hand over her heart. "But not in here."

"Did you minor in psychology?"

"Computer science. With a major in agriscience."

"Then you're completely unqualified to analyze me."

"I supposed you're right," he said to appease her. But qualified or not, he knew hers was a personal search.

She stifled a yawn.

"We need to sleep," he said.

"It's morning already."

"Not quite."

He sidled down the bed, keeping her wrapped in his arms.

"We do need to sleep," she agreed. Then she smiled as she closed her eyes.

Cole sucked in a deep breath. Sleeping with Sydney in his arms. He could get used to this. He shouldn't. She had her career and he had his family.

Still, he could get used to this.

Eyes closed, Sydney waited until Cole's breathing was deep and even. Then she blinked away her fatigue and watched his profile in the gathering light. His tanned skin was stark against the white pillowcase, and she gave into an urge to run her fingertip along his rough chin. She wished she could be honest with him, take him with her, listen to his advice.

For a moment she considered waking him up and swearing him to secrecy. Then she could tell him all about his grandmother's problem, and they could solve it together.

But she couldn't do that. She wasn't even sure Cole would want her to do that. She had a feeling he'd consider a promise to any member of his family to be a sacred trust.

When she was sure he was sound asleep, she carefully inched out of the cradle of his hug and slipped from beneath the covers.

It was 8:00 a.m. in Miami, five in California and seven in Texas. She could only hope that Cole's late night and all those time zone changes would keep him unconscious a few more hours.

She tiptoed into the living room, carefully clicked the French door shut behind her and turned on a small lamp on the desktop. Then she opened her purse and retrieved the number for the Miami fashion show. Hopefully, they'd have contact information for Rupert Cowan.

She dialed the number, spoke to a show coordinator who had Rupert Cowan's business phone number and address. She jotted it down on the hotel notepad, peeled off the sheet and tucked the slip of paper into her purse.

She had no way of knowing if he was the right Rupert Cowan. Heading down there might be a waste of time. But she couldn't for the life of her come up with a way to broach the subject with him on the phone.

She had no choice but to approach him in person and keep her fingers crossed.

She might have one heck of a lot of explaining to do once she got back. But it was time to pull out all the stops. If Rupert Cowan did have the brooch, and if she could get her hands on it, Cole would probably be grateful enough not to question the details.

She unzipped her garment bag, retrieved a blazer and skirt that were only slightly wrinkled, then dressed and headed for the lobby.

When Cole woke up, Sydney was nowhere to be found. She wasn't in the suite. She wasn't in the hotel restaurant. And she wasn't in the lobby.

He knew he had to stop being suspicious of her, but it was unnerving to have her just up and disappear. They were supposed to be working together. Even though he'd promised to give her the benefit of the doubt, he couldn't help but wonder if she was up to something.

Okay, so there was every chance that she was investigating antique dealers, or maybe she'd just gone around the corner. She could easily show up any minute with coffee and bagels.

Still, he glanced around the suite, taking inventory. Her suitcase was open on the sofa. Her toiletries were in the main bathroom. She'd opened a bottle of water at the bar.

What else?

He glanced around for clues.

A pen lay haphazardly across the oak desk next to a hotel note pad. Nothing to say the housekeeping staff hadn't set them out crooked, but nothing to say Sydney hadn't used them, either.

Cole held the notepad up to the light, staring across the fibrous surface. There were a few indentations in the paper, so he took a trick from a television crime drama and shaded across them with a pencil.

Rupert Cowan—2713 Harper View Road. Didn't sound like a deli or a coffee shop to Cole.

Didn't sound like anything, he told himself. She could have a perfectly legitimate reason for writing that down and leaving.

After last night, he was giving her the benefit of the doubt if it killed him.

He crumpled the shaded paper in his fist.

It might even be left over from the last guest.

They'd probably laugh about it later.

He tossed the note into the wastepaper basket and sat down on the couch, bracing his fists on his knees.

He couldn't *wait* to laugh about it later.

Ten

Sydney stepped cautiously into 2713 Harper View Road. Unlike the other commercial businesses on the block, this one had a solid gray door that was tucked into an uninviting little alcove.

Inside, hanging fluorescent lights buzzed in the cavernous space. The shoes of unseen employees shuffled against the gritty concrete floor between rows of beige, Arborite countertops and fabric-filled shelving. A few voices sounded in the distance, and a lone man paged through sketch sheets a few counters back.

"Hello?" Sydney ventured.

The man glanced up, pushing his long, graying hair back from his forehead. "Hey there."

She took a couple steps toward him. "I'm looking for Rupert Cowan?"

The man straightened to about five feet seven. He wore

black slacks and a black, ribbed-knit turtleneck. "You found him."

Butterflies pirouetted in Sydney's stomach. "Oh, good."

He braced his hands against the countertop. "Something I can help you with?"

She moved forward and stretched out her hand. "I'm Sydney Wainsbrook."

He shook. His hand was pale and his grip noncommittal. "Nice to meet you, Sydney."

"I was wondering—" she glanced around, swallowing against her dry throat "—is there somewhere we can talk?"

He laced his fingers in front of his chest. "About?"

"It's a personal matter." Her heart rate was going up, and her palms were getting sweaty.

Thank goodness they'd already shaken hands.

"You looking for a job?" he asked.

Sydney shook her head. "It's... I'd feel better if we could sit down somewhere."

Rupert glanced at his watch. "Well, I'm a little—"

"Please?"

He hesitated. "We could go next door for coffee."

She nodded eagerly. "Perfect."

"Patrice?" Rupert called over his shoulder.

"Yeah?" came a woman's gruff voice from the back of the shop.

"I'm out for a bit. If the agency calls, tell them we'll need all ten girls there by Sunday for rehearsal."

"Okay," came the voice.

Rupert gestured to the door with an open palm.

Sydney gave him a shaky smile, then led the way outside and around the corner, into a small, glass-fronted coffee bar.

"Frappachino? Mochachino?" asked Rupert.

"Let me," said Sydney, pulling out her wallet.

Rupert addressed the clerk. "Small half-caf, two sugars, extra foam."

"Just black for me," said Sydney as she pulled out a few bills.

They took a corner table with a checkered plastic tablecloth and a metal napkin dispenser. The whine of the coffee machine filled the silence.

"Are we through being mysterious?" asked Rupert.

Sydney took a bracing breath. Then, making a firm decision, she opened her purse and took out the picture of the fake Thunderbolt.

"Do you recognize this?" she asked Rupert.

Rupert took the picture between his fingers and sat back in his red leather seat. "You must be one of the Ericksons."

Sydney's stomach bounced clear to the floor.

He *knew* about the Ericksons?

"So, you recognize it?" she asked, struggling to recraft her approach. She hadn't counted on him knowing the story. Did he know about Grandma? About his father? About his mother's extortion?

"It's the heirloom brooch," said Rupert, dropping it on the table top. "My mother warned me you'd come looking for it one day."

If he'd known about the Ericksons, why hadn't he come out of the woodwork before now?

"What, exactly, did she tell you?" asked Sydney.

He stroked his chin as if he'd once had a beard. "You know, you're not what I expected."

"What did you expect?"

The waitress set their coffee cups in front of them, and Rupert shrugged. "Someone a little less classy, a little more West Texas."

"I'm not an Erickson," said Sydney.

"Ah-hh."

She resented his tone. Cole had looked damn classy in his suit yesterday.

"I'm a...friend of the family," she offered. She wouldn't mention the Laurent if she could get away with it. If he thought there was interest from a museum, his price would probably go up.

"And you want the brooch."

She nodded. "I'm prepared to pay."

He shook his head. "Not for sale."

Damn. He was sentimental.

She kept a poker face. "You don't know how much I'm offering."

He propped his elbows on the table and rested his chin on his laced knuckles. "It's pretty valuable to me at the moment."

"For sentimental reasons?"

He let out a cold laugh. "Sentimental? Me? About them?"

"Then, why...?"

He leaned forward. "Ever heard of Thunder Women's Wear?"

Sydney shook her head.

"Don't worry. You will. We caused quite a stir in Miami last season, and we're scheduled for Milan in ten days."

She paused. "I don't understand."

"That little brooch? That stupid little brooch that my mother practically worshiped, is the centerpiece of my new line—the bold, crisp colors, the angular lines, the drama and majesty of it. We reproduced the jewel using embroidery thread and my final model wears the brooch itself in every show."

"A fashion line?"

He nodded. "Years, I've been slaving away in this fashion backwater. Then, one night, I'm hunting through the drawer for a pair of cuff links and out drops the brooch..."

Looking for a pair of cuff links? The man kept the Thunderbolt in his *dresser drawer?*

Sydney was going to have a heart attack right here and now.

He picked some lint from his sleeve. "So, you see. It may not have sentimental value, but it has business value to me."

Sydney took a sip of her coffee, searching her brain for a new tactic. She could blurt out a lucrative price—Grandma had arranged a line of credit. But instinct told her it was too soon to talk numbers.

"Did your mother ever tell you how she got the brooch?"

He cracked a knowing smile. "A gift from dear, old Dad. I figured it was hush money."

"Is that why you never contacted the Ericksons?"

Rupert tipped back his head and laughed. "That would presuppose I gave a damn about his reputation. I just figured those cowpokes would have no more interest in me than I have in them."

Sydney nodded. That was good. If Rupert didn't want anything to do with the family, all the better.

She took another drink of her coffee, choosing her words carefully. "You've probably guessed it has sentimental value to them."

Rupert sipped his frothy brew. "That would be why they sent you."

She nodded, toying with the handle of her mug. "I'm prepared to offer you a hundred thousand dollars."

Rupert didn't react. Not even a flicker.

Sydney swore silently. Maybe he'd had it appraised.

Unexpectedly, the chair beside her squeaked against the floor and a shadow loomed large.

"Whatever she just offered you," said Bradley, plunking himself down and crossing one ankle over the opposite knee. "I'll double it."

Sydney felt like she'd been sucker punched. "How did you…"

He cocked his head. *"Please.* Double-o-seven, you're not."

Sydney could have decked him.

Bradley picked up Sydney's coffee cup and took a deliberate swig. "I assume we're getting down to brass tacks?"

"Who are you?" asked Rupert.

Bradley stuck out his hand. "Bradley Slander. I deal in antiques."

"And I've got a bidding war?" asked Rupert with an impressive air of unconcern.

"If she makes another offer, I'll top that, too." Bradley took another defiant swig of her coffee and slanted her a cold look.

It was official. The man had no soul.

Grandma's line of credit went as high as three hundred thousand. Bradley could easily match that. Even if Sydney added her own savings, there was no way she'd beat him.

"Exciting as this is—" said Rupert, pushing his chair back from the table "—and much as I'd love to add six figures to my bank account today, the Thunderbolt is not for sale."

Sydney reached toward him. "But—"

He stared down his aquiline nose. "Sorry, Sydney."

"Four hundred thousand," said Bradley.

Rupert hesitated.

Sydney swallowed. Should she match it? It would take all of her savings…

"Sorry," said Rupert, taking another step.

Sydney jumped up, nearly knocking over the heavy chair.

She absolutely, positively could not let Rupert out the door without making a deal. Bradley wouldn't give up. He'd be on the phone to Oslo within the hour, upping the ante. He'd eventually win Rupert over, and Grandma would never see the brooch again.

"Really, Rupert—" Sydney began, trying not to gasp for air. "It's a family heirloom."

Rupert shook his head. "And I give a damn, because?"

Should she tell him the truth? That his mother was an extortionist? Put her cards on the table and betray Grandma?

Betraying Grandma would be better than losing the Thunderbolt forever. Wouldn't it?

Her heart was pounding and her palms were sweating. She needed time to think. Somewhere out of the heat, away from that infernal coffee grinder.

Rupert started for the door.

"Wait!" she called in a dry, hoarse voice.

He turned and gave her a salute. "I need it for Milan, Sydney. Milan and beyond."

The fake! The idea slammed into her brain with the force of an anvil.

"I can replace it," she blurted.

He paused with his hand on the knob.

She moved toward him. "I have a replica."

His brow furrowed.

"It's good," she assured him. "It's *very* good. Flawless diamonds, five-carat rubies. You could have the cash *and* the Thunderbolt."

"Half a million," drawled Bradley.

"I'd have to see it," Rupert said to Sydney.

"I'll have it here this afternoon."

Bradley stood up, clattering his chair against the floor. "For half a million you can make two fakes, and then some."

Rupert arched a brow. "Within the week?"

A muscle ticked in Bradley's jaw, and his eyes beaded down to brown dots.

Rupert shook a warning finger at Sydney. "I'll look at it, but it would have to be perfect."

"It's perfect," said Sydney, counting on the fact that the faceted diamonds were only a historical flaw.

He hesitated for a long minute. Then he nodded his head. "Here. Two o'clock. Right now, I have a conference call."

As soon as he disappeared, Sydney groped for her cell phone. Bradley pulled his out of his pocket and left the café. Calling Oslo no doubt. He'd be back with a higher offer this afternoon.

Never mind Norway, thought Sydney as she punched in Grandma's number.

By two o'clock, Cole was forced to face the fact that he'd been duped.

Sydney wasn't coming back. Whatever it was that had brought her flying to Miami must have been a damn good lead. She'd obviously decided she didn't need him anymore, and she'd had no compunction about ditching him.

Maybe she was going to sell the Thunderbolt on the black market. Maybe she'd decided that one big score was worth giving up her career. Maybe she'd never been from the Laurent Museum in the first place.

Lies upon lies upon lies.

Whatever it was she'd decided, it definitely included screwing him.

He stood up from the sofa and crossed the room to retrieve the address from the wastepaper basket. *Twenty-seven thirteen Harper View Road.* There wasn't an explanation in the world that would get her out of this one.

One of Joseph Neely's clerks personally delivered the fake Thunderbolt to the Miami airport. Sydney met him there and made it back to the café with less than five minutes to spare. Where, to her surprise, Rupert pulled out a jeweler's loupe and began inspecting the brooch.

Bradley sat next to her, drumming his fingers against the plastic tablecloth, all traces of his flirtatious persona gone.

"Five hundred and fifty thousand," he ventured, and she knew his profit margin was diminishing. He was going for pride now, pure and simple.

Sydney stared directly into Bradley's eyes. "Four hundred thousand, plus the replica."

Rupert paused, looking up from his inspection. "Will you two *stop*."

The muscle in Bradley's jaw began ticking again.

After an excruciating fifteen minutes, Rupert returned the loupe to his jacket pocket. He closed the case on the fake Thunderbolt, and Sydney held her breath.

Finally, he put his hand out to Sydney, palm up. "Four hundred thousand."

"A cashier's check?" she asked, her heart smacking against her rib cage.

Bradley swore, but Rupert silenced him with a glare.

"A cashier's check will be fine." He pulled a sheaf of papers from his breast pocket. "And you can sign here."

It was Sydney's turn to hold out her hand, palm up.

Rupert smiled his admiration, then he reached into the same pocket and pulled out a worn jewelry case.

She clicked it open, and her entire body shuddered in relief.

"May I?" she asked, pointing to the pocket that held the loupe.

He retrieved it. "Be my guest."

She checked the jewels, then she turned the brooch over to check the casting. A deep sense of satisfaction settled in the pit of her stomach. The Thunderbolt was going home.

She pulled out the envelope containing the two cashiers' checks—one from Grandma's line of credit, the other from Sydney's savings account.

Rupert handed her the pen.

Bradley smacked his fist down on the table.

The transaction was over with surprising speed, and all three of them stood.

"You need an escort to a taxi?" asked Rupert, slanting a glance at Bradley.

Sydney chuckled, enjoying the moment. Glad to have thwarted Bradley, excited about telling Cole, and absolutely thrilled for Grandma.

"I don't think he'll mug me," she answered.

"Man," muttered Bradley. "You're a freakin' lunatic," he said to Rupert.

"It was interesting to meet you, Sydney," said Rupert, ignoring Bradley's pithy comment and striding for the door.

Sydney zipped her purse securely shut and tucked it under her arm.

"Don't look so smug," said Bradley.

"I'm not smug," she returned as they paced for the exit. "I'm happy for the Erickson family."

"Don't you ever gag over all that syrupy sweetness you call a personality?"

Sydney opened the glass door and glanced back at him over her shoulder. "Been nice doing business with you, Bradley." Then she turned her head and took a step, walking straight into Cole's broad chest.

He grabbed her by the upper arms and put her away from him. "You lying, cheating, little—"

"Cole!"

He was dressed like Texas again. A denim shirt, his sleeves rolled up, with faded blue jeans riding low on his hips. His boots gave him an extra inch, and he looked truly dangerous.

He glared past her, eyes hardening on Bradley. "Looks like you changed your mind about slitting your wrists."

No. Oh, no.

Her stomach turned to a block of concrete. She had to explain. She had to make him understand. "It's not—"

Cole shut her up with a look of ice. "Don't even bother."

"But—"

"Do you actually think I'd listen to *anything* you have to say right now?"

Bradley made a move.

"Keep walking," Cole barked, squaring his shoulders and shifting himself between Sydney and Bradley.

Bradley hesitated for a split second. Then he held up his palms and took a step back. "Hey. Nothing to do with me. I've got bigger fish to fry." He turned to walk away.

"Hand it over," Cole demanded in a cold voice.

"You have to let me explain," she pleaded, searching her brain for something that would work as an explanation. She still couldn't give Grandma away.

"Explain?" He laughed coldly. "Explain why you ditched me in a hotel and bought the Thunderbolt for yourself."

"It's not for—"

"You've been stringing me along from the beginning."

"Will you *listen* to me?" What could she say? What would make sense? If only Bradley hadn't shown up. If only Cole had stayed back at the hotel.

He threw up his hands. "I can actually *see* you making up the lies."

"I'm not—" Okay, well, actually, she was.

He shook his head. Then he swiped his thumb across her bottom lip. "As far as I'm concerned, every word that comes out of your pretty little mouth is a lie."

"I never lied to you."

"Yeah? Then what the hell happened to 'Cole. I've got a lead on the brooch. I know who's got it. We can buy it back.' Did I miss that part? Was I not paying attention?"

"It's not that simple."

He folded his arms over his chest, gazing down at her with contempt. "It's *exactly* that simple. Now hand it over before I call the cops."

"You'd have me *arrested?*"

His blue eyes glittered like frozen sapphires. "Damn straight."

"What if—" What could she say? How could she explain it without betraying Grandma?

"You going to give me *another* logical story, Sydney? Been there. Done that." He held out his hand. "Give."

Sydney's shoulders drooped. It didn't matter what she said. It didn't matter what she did. "You've tried, convicted and executed me, haven't you?"

"I may be a little slow on the uptake, but I like to think I'm not a complete idiot."

Sydney yanked the purse from under her arm, fighting back a surge of stinging tears. At least Grandma would have the brooch, she told herself. And Cole would have his inheritance.

She dragged open the zipper. Maybe he would get married someday. Maybe some beautiful bride would give him beautiful children, and he'd pass all the traditions on to them.

She should be happy about that. But she just felt hollow and nauseous as she retrieved the jewel case.

"This the real one?" he asked with a derisive sneer.

She glared at him without speaking.

His voice dropped to a menacing growl as he clicked open the case. "If it's not, you know I'll come after you."

She wasn't about to dignify his accusation. "Tell Grandma…" She stuffed her purse back under her arm, squeezing it down tight. "Tell your grandmother I'm sorry."

His blue eyes hardened to stone in the bright sunshine, and he snapped the case shut. "I don't think so."

Sydney winced.

She'd lost the Thunderbolt. And she'd lost Cole.

Her body suddenly felt too heavy for her frame.

She searched his face, but there wasn't a crack of compassion, no sign of conciliation. Anything she said now would be a waste of breath.

She blinked once, then turned away. She took a couple of wooden steps toward the curb and put up her hand to hail a cab.

Cole didn't call her name, and she didn't look back.

Eleven

Cole wheeled his pickup into a wide spot in front of Grandma's house. The flowers were still blooming. The barns were still standing. And the horses still grazed in the fields.

He'd been to Heaven, then Hell, then home again, but the Texas landscape stuck to its own rhythm, not even missing his presence. He killed the engine, trying to shake the vacant feeling that had built up inside him, forcing himself to drum up some enthusiasm for the good news he was about to give his grandma.

He felt the breast pocket of his shirt for the hard, rectangular package, reassuring himself that the last four days hadn't been a dream—or a nightmare.

He kicked open the driver's door, snapping himself out of his mood. Nobody needed to know he'd been taken for a fool. They only needed to know the brooch was back.

He'd gloss over Sydney's betrayal and gloss over his own gullibility.

He crossed the dirt driveway and took the front stairs two at a time.

"Grandma?" he called as he opened the door.

She appeared in the foyer, wiping her hands on a dish towel. "I heard your truck. Do you have news?"

He forced himself to smile as he slipped the case out of his shirt pocket. "I have great news. I found it."

She searched his face for a moment. "And everything's okay?"

That wasn't exactly the reaction he was expecting. He smiled wider. "Of course it's okay. We have the Thunderbolt." He held the case out to her.

Her pale blue eyes shimmered with tears and she reached for the case, opening it carefully to gaze at the brooch. "Where's Sydney?" she asked, glancing to the open doorway behind him.

Cole inhaled, turning to close the door. "She's in New York."

Grandma stilled. "Why? Why didn't she come home?"

"She had things to do."

"What things?"

"Grandma…"

"What things? Cole Nathaniel? This is her triumph—"

Cole winced and bit back a sharp denial.

"—her achievement—"

He clenched his jaw tight to keep himself silent.

"She needs to be here with us to celebrate."

"Grandma."

"Don't you 'Grandma' me." She snapped the case shut. "She's gone."

"What did you do?"

"Sydney is not our friend," he said as gently as he could.

His grandmother glared up at him, waving the Thunderbolt case. "That's ridiculous. You're marrying her."

Cole ran a hand through his hair, gripping the base of his neck. He needed to get out of here. He needed some air. He needed *not* to be answering questions about Sydney right now. "No, I'm not marrying her."

"Oh, yes, you are." Grandma nodded. "I'm not letting you talk yourself out of this girl. It's time to grow up, Cole. It's time to take on your responsibilities."

"I'll marry someone else. I promise."

Grandma shook her head and clicked her cheeks.

Cole sucked in a breath, calming himself down. The sooner he got it over with, the better. "I didn't want to have to tell you this, Grandma."

"Tell me what? What did you do to that wonderful girl?"

That was it. Cole had had about enough. "That *wonderful girl* tried to *steal the Thunderbolt.*"

"She did not."

Oh, great. Denial. That was helpful. "I watched her do it."

Grandma waved a dismissive hand. "Not possible."

"She's a stranger, Grandma. You can't have such blind faith in her." As Cole had done.

He'd been taken in by her sexy smile and her sultry voice. This was what happened when you started letting emotions mess around with your logic. Or maybe it was his libido that had messed around with his logic.

"She may be a stranger to you, Cole." Grandma tapped the case against Cole's chest. "But I know that woman. She did *not* betray us."

Sydney was amazing, a con artist of incredible talent. She probably duped old people all the time. Her and that partner, Bradley Slander.

"You do *not* know her," said Cole.

"Go get her."

Cole sputtered for a moment. "I will not go get her. Grandma, she ditched me in a hotel room to go and make a deal."

"I'm sure she had a perfectly logical explanation."

"Yeah. It was logical, all right. She wanted to steal the Thunderbolt out from under us."

Grandma waved away his words.

"I waited five hours," he explained. "I took the address from the trash bin. I followed her, and caught her and her partner red-handed, bribing some black market criminal."

The color drained from Grandma's face.

Cole was sorry to disillusion Grandma, but Sydney had to be stopped. She wasn't a good person. She was a thief. "I saw them through the window. The three of them."

"Cole." Grandma's voice turned to a hoarse whisper.

"I'm sorry, Grandma." Nobody wished more than Cole that things had turned out differently. The fake Sydney was one of the most compelling women he'd ever met. Even now, even after everything she'd done to him, he still remembered her laughing voice, her gentle caresses and her emerald-dark eyes. His stomach contracted with regret.

Grandma blinked at him. She gripped the jewel case against her chest. Then she squared her shoulders. "Sit down, Cole. There's something I have to tell you."

Perched on the couch, Cole listened with growing incredulity to his grandmother's confession.

His grandfather?

His *grandma?*

When she got to the part where she'd taken Sydney into her confidence, he jerked up and paced across the room.

With every word, with every passing second, his muscles tightened into harder balls of anger.

He didn't blame Grandma, and he didn't blame Sydney. He blamed his grandfather. And he blamed himself. It was their job to protect the family, to keep them safe.

"She bought it from your half-uncle," Grandma finished. "Then she didn't explain it to you, because I'd sworn her to secrecy. She kept my secret, Cole. She let you hate her, and she kept my secret."

Cole stopped in front of the fireplace mantel, fixing his furious gaze on the picture of his grandfather.

The man was grinning.

Grinning.

Before he was even aware of the impulse, Cole slammed his fist into the wood paneling next to the picture, cracking the veneer, putting four deep dents into the grain.

Strangely, he didn't feel the slightest pain.

"Did I miss something?" came Kyle's voice from the foyer.

A deafening silence swept the room.

"Cole and Sydney had an argument," said Grandma.

"You never punched a wall over Melanie," said Kyle.

As Cole stared at his grandfather, everything inside him turned to stone. Then his chest swelled with an ache, and his throat went raw.

He was just as bad as the old man.

He'd failed.

He wasn't there for Grandma, and he'd sent Sydney packing when he should have been down on his knees thanking her.

She'd done his job for him.

"Cole?" Kyle's voice seemed to come from a long way off. "Any news on the Thunderbolt?"

"It's here," said Grandma, holding out the case.

"Isn't that mission accomplished?" asked Kyle. "So what's wrong?"

What was wrong? Everything was wrong.

A family crisis had unfolded right under Cole's nose, and he hadn't even noticed. And he'd destroyed the woman of his dreams. She was back in New York right now, shutting down the Viking show and killing her career. She didn't deserve this. She'd stepped in to help, and what did she get in return?

He cringed remembering the insults he'd hurled at her on the sidewalk. He'd actually threatened to have her arrested.

And she hadn't said a thing. She'd kept his grandmother's confidence in spite of everything. Everything.

"Cole?" Kyle repeated, moving into the room, all humor gone from his tone.

Cole ignored his brother, slowly turning to meet Grandma's eyes.

When a man could no longer trust his own judgment, what was left? "I don't know what to do," he said.

Grandma took a step forward. "Give her the Thunderbolt."

He shook his head. It was too late. Sydney was canceling the show, and she'd never speak to him again.

"I thought you were marrying her," said Kyle, glancing from one to the other.

"They had a fight," said Grandma. "Get on the next plane, Cole. Go to New York and fix it."

"I can't fix it."

"Yes, you can."

Could he? Would an abject apology help at all? Would the Thunderbolt help, even now?

There was only one way to find out.

Cole straightened.

He filled his lungs.

"What the hell happened?" asked Kyle.

Cole turned on his heel and brushed past his brother. Grandma could tell Kyle, or not tell Kyle about the forgery. Cole would respect her decision. But right now, he had one thing to do, and one thing only.

He banged his way out the door and practically sprinted to the pickup truck.

In her cramped office on the mezzanine floor of the Laurent, Sydney hugged her arms around her chilled body.

"You fell for him, didn't you?" asked Gwen as she perched herself on the window ledge.

Sydney closed her eyes and nodded. At least there was one area where she could be honest with her friend. "I couldn't tell Cole what was really going on, either, and then Bradley showed up…."

"And Bradley's the reason Cole thinks you tried to steal his brooch?"

Sydney nodded again, struggling against the overwhelming weight of defeat. How had Cole found her? How in a city the size of Miami had he happened on that little coffee bar?

She'd thought she was home free. She would have come up with a story, any story. But when she placed the brooch in his hands, he would have known she was on his side.

Instead. Instead…

She groaned out loud. "I wish I could tell you more."

"Hey." Gwen gave a sad laugh. "It's really okay. I don't need to know. But what are you going to tell the boss? He's pretty upset, what with your promises and my promises…"

"That they wouldn't lend it to me, I guess." She shrugged. What did it matter? Her career was over. They were already scrambling to book another show for the front gallery.

Sydney had broken a cardinal rule. She'd made a promise she couldn't keep. She should have called her boss as soon as the brooch went missing. No. She should never have offered it in the first place.

She should never have offered up an item she didn't already have in her hand. But she'd trusted Cole. She knew that if he said he had the Thunderbolt, and he said he'd give her the Thunderbolt, it was as good as done.

Not quite, as it turned out. Not that it was Cole's fault. It was her fault. All her fault.

"Maybe we can replace the Thunderbolt," Gwen suggested. "Use one of the ruby necklaces."

"There's not enough public interest. It had to be a new piece. It had to be a fantastic piece."

"It's not fair that you should get hung out to dry."

Sydney gave a hollow laugh. "It's official. Life's not fair." She knew she should care a lot more about the demise of her career, but she couldn't seem to get past losing Cole.

Every time she closed her eyes, she saw him in the Miami hotel room—the sympathy in his blue eyes when she talked about Nanny and Papa, the twinkle when he fed her a strawberry, and the dark passion when he reached out to touch her hair and pull her in for a kiss.

Stop. She had to stop—

"For the record," came the voice that was haunting her brain, "I gave you the benefit of the doubt."

Gwen's eyes went wide. She quickly slipped down off the window ledge.

Sydney pivoted to see Cole, big as life, lounging against the jamb of her office door.

"I'll...uh..." Gwen quickly brushed past Cole to exit the room.

Sydney blinked, trying to adjust her focus to something that made sense.

"I waited five hours in that hotel room," he said. "It took me *five* hours to convince myself you actually had betrayed me."

"What are you doing here?" Her fingers curled convulsively into the palms of her hands. The Thunderbolt was genuine. He had no excuse to show up and torture her.

He took a couple of steps into the room, swinging the door shut behind him. "Grandma told me."

"Grandma told you what?"

"She told me the truth."

Sydney backed up, shaking her head. That couldn't be. They were home free. Grandma would never have given away her secret once she had the Thunderbolt back.

Sydney's butt came up against her small desk. "No," she whispered.

"Yes." Cole nodded. "Why didn't you tell me, Sydney?"

What kind of a question was that? "I gave her my word. My vow."

"I could have helped you."

"You were the one she was keeping it from."

"She's my responsibility," he snapped.

Sydney recoiled from the shout.

She wished she knew how to help him. This had to be hell on his pride. You took away what a man like Cole needed to protect, and he was lost.

He raked a hand through his hair. "I'm sorry."

"It's okay. I know you're upset."

He moved closer, shaking his head. "No. I'm not sorry I yelled. I mean, I *am* sorry I yelled." He stopped. "But I'm really sorry I mistrusted you. I'm sorry I treated you so badly. I'm sorry we…" His gaze drifted away from hers.

Some of the tension went out of Sydney. "Yeah? Well, I'm sorry about that part, too." They'd played with fire and they'd both been burned. She'd known all along that Cole was temporary, but she hadn't been able to resist him. And now any man she slept with from here on in was going to be held up to his standard.

Even now, his elusive scent teased her.

She shook herself. "Why are you here?"

He hesitated. "I'm here to give you the Thunderbolt."

Her throat went dry. "You can't do that."

"Oh, yes I can."

"But—"

He reached out and took both of her hands.

Her chest contracted with the touch.

"I'm proposing, Sydney."

Her heart skipped a beat. Proposing? For real?

"How do you mean?" she ventured, not daring to believe it could be true. She'd already had that dream crushed once.

"Just like we planned. You show the Thunderbolt. And then…" He shrugged his shoulders and glanced down at the floor.

The faint hope leeched out of her body. "A marriage of convenience, Cole?"

He nodded. "It is the only answer."

She'd once thought so, too. But she'd been wrong. Cole loving her was the only answer. Cole wanting to marry her and spend the rest of his life with her was the only answer she'd accept now.

He'd once asked her if she was ready to walk down the aisle in a white dress, promise to love him, then kiss him, throw a bouquet—and then go their separate ways.

She's been prepared to do it then. She couldn't do it now.

"I don't think it's the answer anymore," she told him, her throat aching with disappointment.

"You've earned it," he said.

She raised her hand to her lips to stifle a bitter laugh. "By lying to you? By sleeping with you?"

"Don't."

She shook her head. "Thanks for the offer, Cole. But I think I'll pass."

She couldn't show the Thunderbolt under these circumstances. And she wasn't even sure she wanted to show it. The brooch was exactly where it was supposed to be, safe with Grandma, safe with Cole, someday safe with Cole's real bride.

"I'm not taking no for an answer," he insisted. "You're the reason we found it. You're the reason we even knew where to look. You were there for Grandma when she couldn't trust me—"

"Oh, Cole." Sydney's heart instantly ached for him. "It wasn't a matter of trust."

"No?"

"She was embarrassed beyond belief. I was a stranger. She didn't care about my opinion the way she cared about yours."

"That's not how I see it."

"You're not thinking clearly."

"I'm thinking perfectly clearly. I want you to marry me. I want you to reap the professional benefits of showing the Thunderbolt. It's all I can offer to make up for…"

Sydney fought the chill that moved over her soul. "I don't want it." Did he think they could just erase the past two weeks? He'd shown her the moon and the stars, then he'd yanked it all away. She'd watched the way he'd treated his family, felt the way he loved them, felt the way life might be if he might have loved her. But he didn't, and he never would, and there was nothing she could do about that.

"You're lying."

"The answer is no, Cole."

"You'll break Grandma's heart."

"Low blow," she retorted, a weak smile cresting his lips.

"You ain't seen nothing yet." He clamped his jaw. "Marry me, or I'll fight dirty."

She folded her arms across her chest, not about to give an inch. "Go ahead. Give it your best shot."

"I'll call Bradley."

Sydney pulled back in horror.

"I'm sure he'll have some ideas about showing the Thunderbolt."

She shook her head. "Cole. No. You don't know what he'll—"

"I'll do it. Either you marry me, or I make a deal with Bradley."

"You're bluffing."

"I don't bluff."

"That man's evil."

"Then marry me."

"No."

He threw up his hands. "I'm not asking you to walk the plank. You only have to put up with me for an hour or two. Give me one little kiss, pretend you like me at the reception, then we each go our own way. You'll find reasons to be in New York. I'll find reasons to be on the ranch. And, after a decent interval, we tell everyone it didn't work out."

"Could a proposal get any less romantic?" she asked.

He glared at her.

"I mean, really, Cole. Is there anything you could add that would make a girl feel less desirable?"

He stared hard into her eyes. "My desire for you was never in question."

Familiar stirrings rose up in Sydney's chest. For a split second she considered saying yes and hauling him off on a real honeymoon. But she couldn't do that. It would only put off the heartbreak, maybe make the pain even worse.

"You're thinking about it," he said. "I can tell you're thinking about it."

She shook her head.

"Say yes, Sydney. You can do it."

Could she?

If she didn't get past her feelings for Cole, she'd go insane. She needed to focus on something else. And her career was the only reasonable distraction. And at least she'd have the satisfaction of thwarting Bradley.

She gazed into Cole's eyes, studied those flecks of storm-tossed gray for the last time.

"Fine," she said, suddenly tired of fighting, tired of feeling, tired of wishing for something he'd never be able to give her. "I'll marry you."

"Yeah?"

"Yeah." She tossed her hair behind her shoulders. "After all, it's the professional coup of a lifetime."

Twelve

Two weeks later Sydney was seriously rethinking her decision to marry Cole. But the Laurent was already poised for the Viking antique show, Grandma had already pinned the Thunderbolt to the bodice of Sydney's wedding gown and, most importantly, Sydney had already said "I do."

In the brand-new hay barn down the driveway from Cole's cabin, all eyes were on the bride and groom. The small band launched into the bridal waltz, and Cole pulled Sydney into his arms.

The floor was rough, and the walls were bare wood. But the acoustics were impressive, and they danced together like they made love together, every movement in sync, every breath in harmony. She could swear their heartbeats had synchronized.

"Relax," he whispered into her ear, gathering her close.

"I'm trying."

"Think about the Thunderbolt," he advised. "You're going to be a very famous woman."

"And so, I'm a success," she said on a forced laugh, fighting to keep it from turning into a tear.

His hand stroked up and down her back, just barely touching her exposed skin where the dress veed between her shoulder blades. Ironic that the very man who was tearing her heart out was also comforting her.

She subconsciously moved closer to the heat of his body, his scent taking her back days and weeks to the tiny bedroom on the shores of Blue Creek. She could almost hear the clock ticking as he messed with time.

He settled his arm more securely across the small of her back while the singer crooned his way through a wholly inappropriate Shania Twain tune.

"Are you remembering?" Cole whispered.

"No," she lied.

He bent closer to her ear, his breath puffing in warm bursts. "I sure am."

"Don't." Memories could kill her. They were killing her.

"No matter what happened," he rasped, swaying to the strains of promises and love for the rest of their lives. "No matter what I said and did that can never be fixed. I want you to know that you rocked my world."

"Cole," she moaned.

"For as long as I live, I'll see you in that billowing bed with strawberry-stained lips and tousled hair, sharing my secrets, looking out for my family."

"Please stop."

"I'm so sorry, Sydney."

She shook her head. "It's not you."

He gathered her closer still. "Well, it's sure as hell not you."

"Maybe it's us."

"Maybe it was circumstances."

She dared to look up at him. "Does it really matter anymore?"

It was over between them. Not that they'd ever had a chance. He was her ticket to the Thunderbolt, nothing more. That he was the lover of a lifetime had messed things up, and that she had to lie to him had messed things up. But even without the lies, without the lovemaking, the best she could have hoped for is exactly where they were now—going into a sham marriage to circumvent a will.

He sighed against the top her head. "I hate leaving things unsettled between us."

"We're settled." She was getting better and better at lying.

"No, we're not."

The band moved into the third chorus, and the lyrics all but pierced Sydney's heart.

"What do you need to settle it, Cole? To know that I'm sorry I lied to you?"

"No." He pulled back, cupping her face in his palms. "That's not what I meant."

To her surprise, he captured her lips in a long, soulful kiss.

Ridiculous hope fluttered to life as the song built to a crescendo of everlasting love.

She pulled back, intent on saving her sanity. "There are two hundred people watching us."

"Lucky them."

"Cole."

"Just tell me you forgive me."

"For what?"

He chuckled softly as the band held the final note. "Right."

"Seriously, Cole. What?"

He stared into her eyes.

The note faded to silence and the audience burst into applause.

Kyle appeared next to Cole's shoulder. "I believe it's the best man's turn."

Cole plucked an ice-cold beer from the bar in the corner of his new barn.

Sydney needed to forgive him for insulting her. She needed to forgive him for threatening to have her arrested. And she also needed to forgive him for not recognizing she was the most wonderful woman on the planet.

He'd picked that sappy song himself, hoping by some miracle she'd know he meant it.

She hadn't.

He briefly acknowledged the congratulations from one of his neighbors, but he didn't engage Clyde in conversation. He wanted to fade into the shadows and watch Sydney sway in Kyle's arms, since tonight might be the last time he saw her.

The song ended and he checked the impulse to rush back to her side.

She glanced around, then glided across the floor, her dress flowing softly around her ankles. A few people stopped her to exchange words, Cole's neighbors, Sydney's co-workers. Then a man cut in front of her, and Cole squinted. He didn't recognize the guest, but something prickled along his spine.

Her back was to him, but her shoulders tensed as the two began to speak. Cole ditched the beer bottle and headed across the floor.

Halfway there, he recognized Bradley Slander.

He swore under his breath and quickened his pace, shouldering his way between guests. He still couldn't see Sydney's expression, but Bradley was way too close.

When Cole got into range, he heard Bradley's tone dripping with malevolence. "—and so I'm wondering what it feels like to whore yourself for an antique."

Sydney recoiled, and something exploded inside Cole's brain. Instinct took over as he crossed the last few yards on a dead run. He grabbed Slander by the collar and slammed him up against the wood wall.

He held him there, nose to nose, forearm jammed against his sternum while Slander's face turned an interesting shade of maroon.

"I don't know how things work up in New York," stormed Cole. "But here in Texas, y'all 've got two choices. You can apologize to my wife and get the hell off my land. Or I can blow off your balls and feed them to the dogs."

Slander's mouth worked, but nothing came out except raspy squeaks.

"Cole?" came Kyle's warning voice.

Cole would have broken Slander's nose for good measure, but he'd already wasted too many minutes of his life on the man, and he needed to make sure Sydney was okay.

He jerked back and let Slander crumple to the floor. Then he turned to look for her.

She stood frozen, a few yards away, her eyes wide as a few people tried to engage her in conversation.

Cole marched to her side and wrapped an arm around her waist, pulling her away from the curious guests.

She was shaking.

Fortunately, the band hadn't seen the altercation, and they played on. He guided Sydney into the middle of the dance floor and gathered her into his arms.

Her glance went to the doorway where Kyle was escorting Slander outside.

Cole turned her so she wouldn't have to look.

Her voice quavered. "He—"

"He sends his apologies," said Cole.

She nodded against Cole's shoulder, her body stiff as a board.

"It's okay," he whispered, rubbing a hand up and down her back. "Relax. It's over. Just dance with me."

She shook her head against his chest. "He just said what they're all thinking."

"No, he didn't."

"That I married you for the brooch."

"They're all thinking you're a beautiful bride."

"They're wondering why you agreed to marry me. They're thinking I'm a mercenary."

"No, they're not."

"That's what Katie thought."

He tipped her chin up. "For a short time, maybe. But then she got to know you. She knows you're not a mercenary."

"But I am." There was a catch in her voice, and his heart ached.

"We both know the truth, and that's all that matters."

She shook her head once more.

He kissed the softness of her hair. "Stop. Just stop."

"But we don't, Cole."

"We don't what?"

She tilted her chin to look up, eyes glassy and tearful. "*You* don't know the truth."

He squinted at her. Oh, no.

"The truth is, I didn't marry you for the brooch."

A chill of fear iced Cole's spine. He couldn't take another one of her deceptions. Not here. Not now.

She bit her bottom lip, and her chest rose once, then fell. "I married you because I love you."

The fear in Cole's body plummeted through the floorboards. He gave his head a little shake. She couldn't have just said those words. It was his own wishful thinking.

"Say that again," he rasped, fighting the roaring in his ears.

"I love you, Cole," she repeated.

He squeezed her tight. "Oh, Sydney. I have loved you for..." He stroked his hand slowly over her fragrant hair, marveling that his dreams had actually come true. "Forever, I think."

Her voice lifted. "You do?"

He kissed her temple. "I do."

A soft sigh escaped from her, she seemed to melt against him.

"Oh, Cole.

"I know."

"We're married."

"I meant the song." He cradled her face in his hands. "For as long as I live. I meant every word."

"I meant my vows," she whispered.

"I will love you," he whispered back, "cherish you, honor and keep you."

"Till death do us part," she said, finding his hand with her own and twining their fingers together.

"Till death do us part," he repeated, pulling their joined hands between their bodies as the music swelled. The yellow lights shone through her hair and the scent of the wedding roses filled the new barn.

"I guess we'll be building that house now," said Cole, feathering light kisses down her cheek, heading for her soft lips.

"With the turret and the dormer windows." She sighed against him. "And a breakfast bar and some of those high stools with the curved backs."

He chuckled. "I guess if I'm going to be a patriarch, I'll need a big house."

"A patriarch?"

"Yeah."

"Oh, great. You're going to start issuing decrees now, aren't you?"

"You bet." He nodded. "Starting tonight, I'm whipping this family into shape."

"Kyle will never take the land."

"I know he won't." Cole smiled to himself. He'd been working on that one for a while.

"What?" Sydney prompted.

"I'm leaving it to his children."

"You're devious."

"That I am. But you love me, right?"

"I love you," she said.

"Say it again."

She pulled back and cupped his face between her soft hands. "I love you, Cole Erickson."

He sighed. He could listen to that all night long.

"Isn't there something you want to say to me?" she prompted.

He kissed her softly on the lips. "Hmm. Let me think."

She dug her elbow into his ribs.

"I love you Sydney…Erickson," he rumbled.

A funny expression flitted across her face.

"I guess we didn't talk about names, did we?" He wasn't going to insist. After all, traditions had to change sometime.

"Sydney Erickson." She rocked her head back and forth. "I think I like that." Her lips curved into a smile.

Cole grinned right back, smoothing her hair, kissing her again. They could have a real honeymoon now. He'd planned to hide out in Montana for a week, but he'd go wherever she wanted.

"Hey, Cole." Kyle danced up to them with Katie in his arms.

Cole nodded to his brother, hugging Sydney close.

"Who was that guy?" Katie asked Sydney.

"Antique vulture," Sydney answered, and Cole was proud of how quickly she'd recovered from the altercation.

"Won't *ever* be back to the Valley," said Kyle.

Cole nodded his thanks. He should've broken Slander's nose. But then the sheriff might have had to lock him up on his wedding night.

"Thought you two might like to know the wedding worked," said Katie with a wide smile.

"Sure did," said Cole, though he wasn't sure how Katie knew that already. He kissed Sydney's temple.

"Looks like along about April," said Katie.

Sydney let out a sudden squeal and pulled away from Cole's arms.

"What?" asked Cole as his wife embraced his sister-in-law.

"New little Erickson," said Kyle with wide, sappy grin.

Cole let out a whoop. He reached out and clapped Kyle on the shoulder. "That's fantastic! Congratulations, little brother."

"Thanks," said Kyle.

"Can we talk about splitting the land now?" asked Cole.

"No," said Kyle.

Cole smiled as he shook his head. "I'm going to win this one."

Someone tapped his shoulder and he turned.

"Hey, Grandma." He pulled Sydney back into his arms as Kyle danced off with Katie. "Don't you just love a good wedding?"

"You know I do," said Grandma. "And I have something for Sydney."

Sydney tipped her head questioningly. "For me?"

"This way," said Grandma with a mysterious wink. "Both of you."

They followed her through the crowd, past the band, toward the back of the barn where the light was dim and the air was a few degrees cooler.

Cole held Sydney's hand as they walked, unable to resist sending goofy smiles her way. He couldn't wait to get her alone.

Or maybe he could. It was fun to show her off. His wife. His *wife*. And tonight was the first of thousands together.

Yeah, he could wait.

He lifted her hand to his lips and kissed each of her knuckles. He was going to relish every single hour with this woman.

Grandma came to a stop at a back table, rattling something out of a paper bag.

She turned to face Sydney with a very serious expression on her face. "Sydney Erickson."

Cole squeezed Sydney's hand. He loved her new name.

"It is my honor," said Grandma, "to present you with the providence and chronicles of the Thunderbolt of the North." She handed Sydney a large, leather-bound book.

Sydney's forearms sagged with the weight of the dark, heavy volume. Cole started to take it from her, then checked the impulse. Her eyes were wide with wonder as she stared down.

Cole blinked in amazement as well. He hadn't even known such a thing existed.

"It was translated in the mid-1700s," said Grandma, patting her hand gently on the cover. "I've never been sure if it was taken from a written account, or if Sigrid wrote down the oral history. In any event, it's all here. The life and times of the Thunderbolt."

Sydney ran her fingers over the embossed cover. "This is absolutely amazing," she whispered, glancing up at Cole. "It's priceless."

Grandma smiled with obvious satisfaction. "And it's your turn to continue the saga."

Sydney's jaw dropped open.

"And I suggest you start with the Thunderbolt's latest adventure."

"Are you sure?" asked Sydney. "The *entire* adventure?"

Grandma patted the book again. "Yes. The whole adventure. The diary deserves no less than the truth."

Cole wrapped an arm around his grandmother's thin shoulders and gave her an affectionate squeeze. "Thank you, Grandma."

Her eyes shimmered bright as she smiled up at him.

"For everything," he said.

"I was right about Sydney, wasn't I?"

"You were absolutely right about Sydney."

"Good. Well, I'll leave you two alone now," she said with a quick smile.

"I can't believe it," said Sydney, her voice hoarse with awe.

"It couldn't be in better hands," said Cole, loving her more by the second.

She shook her head, and her eyes shimmered jewel-bright under the lights. Then she pressed the big book more tightly against her chest. "I never thought it could happen," she whispered. "But you did it, Cole."

"I did what?" He searched her eyes. "I fell in love with you?"

She shook her head. "That, too." Then she reached up

and stroked her soft palm against his cheek. "What I meant was, you found my silver locket."

Ah. His gaze went to the brooch, nestled against the beaded fabric of her wedding dress. "The Thunderbolt."

She shook her head again. "No. It was never the jewelry." She smiled. "It was never the things."

"Then…"

"It was the heritage, the home. I finally realized." She swayed toward him, and his arms automatically wrapped around her.

"I was searching for the family I never had. And you gave it to me."

His chest expanded almost painfully.

She was his. She was here forever.

"Welcome home, Sydney," he whispered against her hair. "We've been waiting for you all along."

* * * * *

Silhouette
Desire

COMING NEXT MONTH

#1705 TAKING CARE OF BUSINESS—Brenda Jackson

The Elliotts

How far will an Elliott heir go to convince a working-class woman that passion is color-blind?

#1706 TEMPT ME—Caroline Cross

Men of Steele

He is the hunter. She is his prey. And he's out to catch her at any cost.

#1707 REUNION OF REVENGE—Kathie DeNosky

The Illegitimate Heirs

Once run off the ranch, this millionaire now owns it…along with the woman who was nearly his undoing.

**#1708 HIS WEDDING-NIGHT WAGER—
Katherine Garbera**

What Happens in Vegas…

She left him standing at the altar. Now this jilted groom is hell-bent on having his revenge…and a wedding night!

#1709 SEVEN-YEAR SEDUCTION—Heidi Betts

Would one week together be enough to satisfy a seduction seven years in the making?

#1710 SURROGATE AND WIFE—Emily McKay

She was only supposed to have the baby…not *marry* the father of her surrogate child.

SDCNM0106